The First Book of
Old Mermaids Tales

Also by Kim Antieau

Old Mermaids Books

The Blue Tail • *Church of the Old Mermaids* • *The First Book of Old Mermaids Tales* • *The Fish Wife* • *An Old Mermaid Journal* • *The Old Mermaids Book of Days and Nights* • *The Old Mermaids Book of Days and Nights: A Year and a Day Journal* •*The Old Mermaids Oracle* • *The Second Book of Old Mermaids Tales*

Other Novels

Broken Moon • *Butch* • *Coyote Cowgirl* • *Deathmark* • *The Desert Siren* • *Her Frozen Wild* • *The Gaia Websters* • *Jewelweed Station* • *The Jigsaw Woman* • *Maternal Instincts* • *Mercy, Unbound* • *The Monster's Daughter* • *Queendom: Feast of the Saints* • *The Rift* • *Ruby's Imagine* • *Swans in Winter* • *Whackadoodle Times* • *Whackadoodle Times Two*

Other Nonfiction

Answering the Creative Call • *Certified: Learning to Repair Myself and the World in the Emerald City* • *Counting on Wildflowers: An Entanglement* • *The Salmon Mysteries: a Reimagining of the Eleusinian Mysteries* • *The Salmon Mysteries Workbook: Reimagining the Eleusinian Mysteries* • *Under the Tucson Moon*

Other Collections

Entangled Realities (with Mario Milosevic) • *Haunted* • *Tales Fabulous and Fairy* • *Trudging to Eden*

Chapbook

Blossoms

Blog

www.kimantieau.com

Photography

www.kimantieau.smugmug.com

The First Book of Old Mermaids Tales

Kim Antieau

Green Snake PUBLISHING

The First Book of Old Mermaids Tales
by Kim Antieau

Copyright © 2011 by Kim Antieau

ISBN-13: 978-1-949644-06-7

All rights reserved.

www.kimantieau.com

No part of this book may be reproduced
without written permission of the author.

Cover photos by Kim Antieau.
Design by Mario Milosevic.
Special thanks to Nancy Milosevic.

Published by Green Snake Publishing
www.greensnakepublishing.com

*For
Joanna and Cate*

Contents

Introduction

I HAVE MERMAIDS all over my house. They swim in and out of every room. Most of them were gifts. I think the only mermaids I actually bought are the two wooden mermaids I got at the Flea in Santa Fe, one of which graces the covers of *Church of the Old Mermaids* and *An Old Mermaid Journal.*

I wasn't a mermaid kind of kid. I lived in the Midwest in a small town with lots of lakes. I don't remember even thinking about mermaids. Whenever I saw depictions of mermaids, they seemed like sexual objects more than anything else, with perky breasts and long flowing hair. They didn't correspond with my idea of a powerful female image. (When I was a girl, I had an entire imaginary world where the girls and women had magical powers and the boys and men did not. The men were respected and held in high esteem because they were the homemakers, but they had no actual power. So even as a girl, I understood iconic images.)

My ideas of mermaids changed as I began studying goddess lore some years ago. The first goddesses were (most likely) primal sea goddesses, often depicted with fish tails. The ancient oracular mermaid goddess Atargatis slipped into our world via a heavenly egg. Atargatis may have been related to Aphrodite (mythologically speaking). I liked imagining Aphrodite rising up from the sea as a powerful life and death goddess with a fish tail. I preferred this to the image of her on a seashell trying to cover up her naked body.

When I first saw an artist's depiction of the great Yoruba goddess Yemaya rising out of the ocean with two tails, I finally understood the power of the mermaid. She was no "little" mermaid, looking for a man. She was an ancient sea goddess, potent and powerful. She had not been diminished through time; she had not been stripped of her power or stories.

Even as I learned more about mermaids, I didn't write about them. When I was in my thirties, a friend showed me the painting "Village of the Mermaids" by the surrealist artist Paul Delvaux. I was captivated by it. Eight Victorian women are depicted on a village street, sitting in chairs outside a row of houses on either side of the road. The women are completely covered except for their heads and hands. They each have long hair, and they stare straight ahead, without emotion. A man is walking away from them, toward the ocean. Beyond them and their village, in the distance, we can see the beach and the ocean where eight mermaids swim and sunbathe.

I felt haunted by this painting for years. I wrote a story called "Village of the Mermaids." I can't remember anything about it except that it wasn't very good. I had a poster of the painting on my wall for years, but I finally threw it out. All I could see when I looked at it were the depressed women in the village. I wasn't able to see—truly—the mermaids beyond them, heading out to the Old Sea and freedom.

Years later, in 2006, my husband Mario and I were at a writing retreat in Tucson, AZ, beginning a novel. (Many of you who have read *Church of the Old Mermaids* and my blog have heard this story before.) I had just read *The Old Man and the Sea* again, and I wanted to write a female version of that story: a simple tale, showing a woman's power and relationship with the world. I sat in this tiny 8 x 10 room in the Sonoran desert, trying to think of an idea for *The Woman and the Old Sea*.

I could hear the sounds of the desert beyond the open door, could see the blue sky, feel the dry air against my skin. I imagined a woman walking in a wash (much like the wash running through the property where I was retreating), picking up garbage. I knew right away she would sell the interesting trash she found.

In years past, we had sometimes seen a man selling what looked like found items on 21st street in Portland. In my memory, he put these objects on a table and called this table "The Church of Elvis." I could have gotten this wrong because there is actually a museum/gallery called the Church of Elvis in Portland; according to his wiki entry, he never sold trinkets on 21st street in Portland. The reality of it doesn't matter. I thought of the Church of Elvis as I sat in the desert, and I wondered what my character, Myla Alvarez, would call her "church" table. Almost immediately the Old Mermaids started coming to me. It was as if they walked out of the wash and began telling me their stories. In my memory, that is exactly what happened.

Church of the Old Mermaids was born.

Thirteen Old Mermaids walked out of the Old Sea and into the New Desert and had to create new lives and community.

And I got to tell their stories.

I was at the writing retreat for a month and I finished the novel before we left. That spring I had two surgeries, and I felt like the Old Mermaids came with me and protected me during this time. I have written stories since I was five years old. I have loved and admired most of my characters. This was the first time that characters in one of my stories became guides or helpers in my life. I feel like I now have thirteen fairy goddessmothers.

Yet when I look back at my life, I wonder if they have always been a part of it. When I was nineteen, I was depressed and tried to kill myself. Afterward, I went to live in a tiny attic apartment by myself. I don't remember saying a word for nearly a year. I'm sure I did because I had a job and I was going to school. But I don't remember having a conversation with anyone. During this time, I occasionally wondered if I was ever going to feel better—or feel anything at all. Then one night I dreamed that a watery being came to me.

In the dream I thought of her as a water dryad—a water nymph. She was beautiful. She had huge soulful eyes. Water and seaweed ran up and down her whole body and through her hair. We made love all night long. When I woke up the next morning, I knew I would be all right. And I was. I slowly but markedly began to come out of my depression.

Later I realized she must have been a naiad, a kind of river mermaid.

So perhaps the Old Mermaids have been with me for a

long while.

In any case, I'm happy they're with me now. I feel as though knowing them and telling their stories has enriched and saved my life. I'm happy to be able to share these stories of the Old Mermaids with the world. They are all healing tales, I believe. For me, they are a balm when I'm feeling inflamed by the world.

This first volume of *Old Mermaids Tales* has excerpts from my novels *Church of the Old Mermaids* and *An Old Mermaid Sanctuary*, stand-alone stories about the Old Mermaids, and some other goodies from the Old Mermaid Sanctuary.

I hope you enjoy.

Blessed sea!

—*Kim Antieau*

Grandmother Yemaya Mermaid and the Thirteen Quilts

SOME TIME AFTER the Old Sea dried up and the Old Mermaids washed up on the shores of the New Desert, Grand Mother Yemaya Mermaid decided she wanted to find a way to comfort the Old Mermaids who were far from home and lonesome for Old Friends and the Old Sea.

It wasn't that the Old Mermaids weren't happy in the Old Mermaid Sanctuary creating their home and making new acquaintances with the furred, the flying, and the friendly. Still, Grand Mother Yemaya Mermaid had seen the tears and heard the longing in the voices of the Old Mermaids when they spoke of their life before the New Desert. Grand Mother Yemaya Mermaid was the oldest of the Old Mermaids after all, and she wanted to gift the Old Mermaids with something that would bring them comfort all the days and all the nights.

Grand Mother Yemaya Mermaid began wandering the wash and thereabouts looking for those things which would bring the Old Mermaids comfort. Now this you probably already know, but I will say it again: Grand Mother Yemaya Mermaid was the wisest of the wisest of the Old Mermaids. She had known the Old Sea was drying up long before anyone else. She knew the paths of the stars in the Old Sky. She knew the difference between the smell of rain and the smell of snow, even before she had ever seen snow. She knew the languages of the birds and the bees and the winds and the trees. And she could sit with Old Woman and Old Man of the Mountains and discuss the affairs of the mountains, desert, rivers, and forests with clarity, humor, and insight—as though Old Woman, Old Man, and Grand Mother Yemaya Mermaid had been friends since the beginning of time. And perhaps they had been.

So Grand Mother Yemaya Mermaid understood that "things" would not make the Old Mermaids happy. Still, she knew that each place had a way of being, a natural flow, a kind of enchantment about it. And the Old Mermaids needed help finding the flow of this seemingly still and prickly New Desert, they needed help discovering the enchantments of the New Desert, and just maybe a found object from their new world would help with this.

Grand Mother Yemaya Mermaid did find all sorts of objects in the New Desert: rocks, feathers, bones, and wood. She let it all be. While each object was beautiful and profound in its own way and Grand Mother Yemaya Mermaid could have spent forever out in the desert admiring and contemplating each piece, none of them was quite what she needed for the

                              The First Book of

Old Mermaids.

One day, Grand Mother Yemaya Mermaid came upon the home of Louie, the Man Who Collects, and Betty, the Woman Who Weaves. Louie and Betty had been to the Old Mermaid Sanctuary many times. Louie had a standing invitation to sample Sister Ruby Rosarita Mermaid's soups since he was somewhat of a soup connoisseur himself. Louie could smell one of Sister Ruby Rosarita Mermaid's soups before she even started one, so Grand Mother Yemaya Mermaid often saw him in the sanctuary.

This day, Louie, the Man Who Collects, greeted Grand Mother Yemaya Mermaid and asked her in for lunch. Betty, the Woman Who Weaves, was not at home so Louie and Grand Mother Yemaya Mermaid sat together and ate squash soup, mostly in silence, listening to the other sip the deep golden liquid.

When they were finished, Grand Mother Yemaya Mermaid said, "Sometimes it feels as though we are far far from home. But today is not one of those days."

"What brings you to this part of the desert?" the Man Who Collects asked.

"I was looking for something that would comfort the Old Mermaids when they are feeling homesad."

Louie, the Man Who Collects, nodded. "That reminds me of the story of Betty's comforter. She knows the story better than I do, since it happened to her. But she is out today with the other weavers, coaxing string and thread from desert plants. She's spent her whole life in this desert. She grew up not far from here, you know. This desert can be harsh. Her parents were very poor, and one year they had not had rain for a longer while than usual and things were going badly for them. Betty's clothes were threadbare. She didn't even have a blanket to keep her warm on those cold desert nights. This went on for some time.

"Then one night Betty remembers waking up and hearing her mother and father out under the moon, over by an agave plant, singing and rattling and praying. She fell back to sleep the way children do. She couldn't be sure, but she thinks it was the next morning when she awakened feeling warm and comforted. She lay in her bed savoring this wonderful feeling for several minutes before she realized she was covered in a quilt. She pulled it off and looked at it. It looked as though someone had sewn pieces of the desert together with an almost translucent blue thread: leaves, prickly pear pads, bones, feathers. Yet when she touched it, it was cloth—beautiful, soft, warm cloth.

"She ran out to the kitchen where her parents were making breakfast. She thanked them for the quilt. 'You are welcome, daughter,' her mother said, 'but it was Grandmother Spider who answered our prayers. It is her thread that holds the pieces of desert together in your comforter. It would be good if you went out and thanked her.' Betty ran to the agave plant, where she saw a small pale blue green spider weaving a web between the thick succulent agave leaves. And curling off these leaves were strands of thread the same color as the plant and the spider. Betty thanked Grandmother Spider. It was that day she decided to become a weaver."

Grand Mother Yemaya Mermaid and Louie sat in silence

     The First Book of

for a time. Then Grand Mother Yemaya Mermaid said, "You have solved my problem, Louie. I will make thirteen desert comforters for the Old Mermaids. Thank you."

"You are welcome," he said. "I have thread if you would like it. I've collected it from here and there, and Betty has given me some from Grandmother Spider. Betty taught me how to make quilts long ago."

"So you've made them yourself! How grand. Do you have any advice for me?"

"Focus," he said. "That's important. Think of each quilt as a puzzle. And of course, sing to the thread and the desert as you're sewing."

"Of course," she said.

Louie, the Man Who Collects, got up and retrieved a pale blue cloth bag and handed it to Grand Mother Yemaya. Inside was a ball of nearly translucent blue thread.

"Come by the Old Mermaid Sanctuary soon," Grand Mother Yemaya Mermaid said. "Sister Ruby Rosarita Mermaid is cooking up some kind of feast."

"I knew it," he said. "I told Betty something was cooking at the sanctuary."

Grand Mother Yemaya Mermaid was excited by the prospect of creating thirteen comforters for the Old Mermaids. It is said—though I can't be sure if it's true—that she began as soon as she left Louie's house by asking the Invisibles of the place if she could please find and pick up pieces of the desert for the quilts. And so she gathered up leaves from the mountains and forests. She found branches there, too, and the bones of many creatures. She gathered feathers and the whispers of dreams on her way down. On the floor of the desert, she found prickly pear pads and the skeletons of cacti. She gathered up the clucking of the quail and the hooting of the owl. She found flat rocks, more feathers, and the songs of coyotes. One day she found seashells in the wash. She kept looking until she had thirteen. Finally she sat under the night sky and caught the dust of falling stars. She scooped up moonlight at the same time.

Grand Mother Yemaya Mermaid spread what she had found all around her. They say these found pieces went on for miles. But Grand Mother Yemaya Mermaid knew where everything was. When it was time, she began singing to the thread and calling on Grandmother Spider for her assistance. Sister Laughs A Lot and Sister Lyra Musica Mermaids were watching from a near distance, and they told the others that the thread began glowing then, as though it was made from moonlight. Sister Laughs A Lot and Sister Lyra Musica Mermaids loved a good story as much as any Old Mermaid, so it's possible the thread never glowed. It's even possible that Grand Mother Yemaya Mermaid never sang—but I doubt it. I am guessing she sang the entire time she sat on the desert floor stitching those pieces of desert into quilts. This leaf went with that feather and that feather went with the sound of the singing stream and the singing stream went with the bones of the cholla and the bones of the cholla went with the dreams of the Old Mermaids and the dreams of the Old Mermaids went with the star dust and the star dust went with the seashells and the seashells went with the purr of the bobcat. And on and on.

                              The First Book of

After a while, Grand Mother Yemaya Mermaid stopped singing and began weaving love and healing and nourishment and comfort into the quilts. "May you never know hunger," she said. "May you know great joy. May you be filled up with love. May you dance and laugh. May you know the touch of moonlight on your brow. May you know the love of a good man. May you know the love of a good woman. May you know the love of children. May you know the love of the stars, and the moon, and the sun. May you know the peace of a blue sky. May you have the curiosity of a crow. May you have the happiness of an Old Sea or New Desert full of Old Mermaids."

A day or a week or a month or a lifetime later, Grand Mother Yemaya Mermaid completed the quilts. As she gazed at them covering the desert floor, she wondered—for just a second—how these rough prickly pieces of the desert were ever going to bring comfort to anyone. She thanked Grandmother Spider and all the creatures of the New Desert. She picked up the quilts one by one, and carefully folded them. By the time she was finished, it was night and all the Old Mermaids were asleep. She took the quilts into the house and to each Old Mermaid. Every quilt was made from different pieces of the desert, of course, and Grand Mother Yemaya Mermaid had sewn a little extra into each one.

Grand Mother Yemaya Mermaid laid a quilt over Sister Sheila Na Giggles Mermaid and whispered, "I sewed the strength of an eagle into your quilt."

"And into yours I sewed the beauty of moonlight and sunlight wrapped around one another," she whispered to Sister

DeeDee Lightful Mermaid.

As she dropped the comforter over Sister Bea Wilder Mermaid, she said, "Into yours I sewed the magic of the bobcat, the mountain lion, and the lynx."

She whispered to Sister Faye Mermaid, "Into yours I sewed knowledge of peace and desert magic."

"Into yours I sewed a falling star," Grand Mother Yemaya Mermaid whispered to the sleeping Mother Star Stupendous Mermaid, "and the sound of the Old Sea."

To Sister Magdelene Mermaid, she said, "Into yours, I sewed the love of the mountains, desert, and sky."

For Sister Sophia Mermaid, she said, "Into yours I sewed the wisdom of the New Desert."

"Into yours, I sewed the nourishment of the Old Sea," she told Sister Ruby Rosarita Mermaid.

"Into yours, I sewed the poetry of the stars and the moon," she whispered to a sleeping Sister Bridget Mermaid.

To Sister Ursula Divine Mermaid, she said, "Into yours I sewed all the knowledge of the wild things."

"Into yours," she told Sister Laughs A Lot Mermaid, "I sewed the hugs of a forest full of giants."

And to Sister Lyra Musica Mermaid, she said, "Into yours, I sewed the music of the stars."

It is said that as Grand Mother Yemaya Mermaid draped each quilt over a sleeping Old Mermaid, the quilt changed, softening and shifting until it was more than pieces of the New Desert sewn together; each became the yielding healing cloth Grand Mother Yemaya Mermaid had intended it to be. And from that day forward, the Old Mermaids needed only

　　　　The First Book of

to wrap themselves in their quilts to feel comfort, to feel more like themselves, to recall the Old Sea without sorrow, to feel wrapped up in sunlight and moonlight and the breath of giants and the mystery of the Invisibles—to know the songs of coyotes and the mystery of desert faeries. It was a great gift Grand Mother Yemaya gave to the Old Mermaids.

About the time Grand Mother Yemaya Mermaid finished giving the comforters to the Old Mermaids, it was dawn. The Old Mermaids began awakening. Each of them gathered the soft beautiful comforters around them and went outside to watch the sun come up and to ooh and ahh over their new quilts. Grand Mother Yemaya Mermaid smoothed her hand down over each quilt, hardly believing what had happened herself. She was just about to unfold the thirteenth quilt and put it over her shoulders when Louie, the Man Who Collects, came hurrying up to them.

"I am sorry to come so early," he said, "but we were out collecting and found something in the wash that we think you should see."

The Old Mermaids followed Louie into the wash. They walked a long while until they saw Betty, the Woman Who Weaves, waiting for them. The sun came up over the ridge just then, spreading golden light across the desert, giving everything a gold and red halo. The Old Mermaids gathered around Betty and looked at what lay at her feet.

They were the bones of an Old Mermaid.

Grand Mother Yemaya Mermaid and Mother Star Stupendous Mermaid thanked Louie and Betty. They nodded and left the Old Mermaids alone.

"I wonder who," Sister Laughs A Lot Mermaid said.

"When?" Sister Magdelene Mermaid asked.

"When the Old Sea dried up," Sister Sophia Mermaid said. "When else."

"What should we do?" Sister Lyra Musica Mermaid asked.

"Take her back," Sister Faye Mermaid said. "Back to the Old Sea."

"If we could do that," Sister Bea Wilder Mermaid said, "we'd take ourselves back." The Old Mermaids were silent. "Wouldn't we?"

"They say the Big River flows into what's left of the Old Sea," Grand Mother Yemaya Mermaid said. "Let's take her there."

The other Old Mermaids agreed. Grand Mother Yemaya Mermaid unfolded the quilt she had carried under her arm and she laid it on the desert floor. The others carefully picked up the bones of the Old Mermaid and put them on the comforter. Grand Mother Yemaya Mermaid folded the cloth up around the bones. Then she lifted the bundle into her arms. The Old Mermaids began walking. Sister Bridget Mermaid and Sister Faye Mermaid began singing sea chanties, and soon the others joined it. Then they started the encouragements: "You'll be home soon, Sister Mermaid." "Oh, you'll be in the Old Sea in no time." "Say hello to everyone for us." "It'll be a grand time." And then they sang some more.

When they reached the shores of the Big River, it was near night. Grand Mother Yemaya Mermaid stepped forward, a bit away from the other Old Mermaids, and looked down

The First Book of

at the rushing water. The Old Mermaids sang softly near her, their desert comforters wrapped tightly around them. Grand Mother Yemaya Mermaid said, "May you be, may you be, may you be," and she slowly began unwrapping the quilt.

I can't be sure of what happened next. I can only tell you what was told to me. But as she unwrapped the thirteenth quilt to drop the bones of the Old Mermaid into the river, the bones slipped away on their own. Only they weren't bones. Some say a salmon twisted out of the quilt and leaped into the water. Some say a faery slid away. Still others say it was the Old Mermaid herself, restored to life. The Old Mermaids didn't know what happened. It was dark. Grand Mother Yemaya Mermaid was so startled, she dropped the quilt. It fell right into the river and disappeared along with the salmon or the faery or the New Old Mermaid.

The Old Mermaids began clapping and cheering and laughing and dancing in the moonlight and river light. Everyone says that you could see their tails flashing like a thousand tiny colored moons. Or gills on a fish. You take your pick.

Sometime later, the Old Mermaids walked home to the Old Mermaid Sanctuary. Once there, each of the Old Mermaids cut off a piece of her quilt. They sewed all the pieces together with the blue thread so that Grand Mother Yemaya Mermaid had her own quilt.

The Old Mermaids kept their quilts close to them for maybe as long as the mountains stood. Some say once the quilts began falling apart from use and wear, the Old Mermaids sewed new comforters from the bits and pieces of the old quilts. Oh, the stories I could tell you about those new old quilts. They say that any piece or strand of thread from those first quilts used in any other quilt carried forward all the healing qualities of the first, only more so, even today.

And what about that thirteenth quilt that fell into the Big River? Some say it went all the way to the ocean. Others say a whale swallowed it and someone named Jonah used it as a blanket. Most people believe the quilt survived. They say if you use a patch of the thirteenth quilt in any other quilt you better be prepared for change. It could turn you into a salmon, a desert faery, or an Old Mermaid. If you find any of it, sew it into a quilt and see what happens. If you dare.

From The Old Mermaids Journal: Rattleday

I T IS SO quiet. I hear the wind lifting the dry palm leaves and shaking them. It sounds a bit like the rattle Sissy Maggie Mermaid made out of a dried gourd one year. Only bigger. It was a storm rattle. Sissy Maggie stood outside with that rattle and danced for a long while, until a Storm did come to see what all the noise was about. The desert breathed moist that night.

I know the Old Owl is hidden up in the green leaves of the palm, but I cannot see him from where I sit.

I wonder where the others are. For a moment. Then I continue to relish the silence. A tiny whirring bird dips her long beak into one of the pink flowers near the palm tree. Annie, the Woman Who Loves Birds, calls them hummingbirds. I have never heard them hum, only whir.

They are fierce birds. Flecks of the moon, sun, and stars make their feathers iridescent. One of the whirring birds is the color of the mountains. I believe he must know the Old Man and Old Woman of the Mountains.

Annie is the one who gave us this journal to record our daily lives at the Old Mermaid Sanctuary. This does not come natural to most of the Old Mermaids. We don't need a record of the ongoing conversations we have with ourselves and the world. We've kneaded these conversations into our home, our friendships, the land, our community.

Oh look. This whirring bird has a throat the color of the night sky in summer. I wonder how he convinced the Old Sky to part with those pieces of night. Probably with the same determination that the others used to get pieces of the sun, moon, and stars. Ah, but who would not want to be a decoration at the throat of such a being?

The cover of the journal is made of red-cloth with white and pink stitching. I am not much for words, although the others often seek my advice. I believe the world is always whispering an enchantment to us—to all that exists. Too many useless words might interfere with this magic and then who knows what might unravel?

We must choose our words, our songs, our enchantments carefully so that we are not generating a cacophony but instead toning with the universe, singing a kind of creation lullaby.

Now the mourning birds have come for their daily drink and bath. I had not realized it was so late in this day. I will sit here and watch them. Perhaps I will tell this journal about it another day.

Ahhh, listen to the palm rattle. Someone is dancing up a storm somewhere.   *—Mother Star Stupendous Mermaid*

                                    The First Book of

Sister Sophia Mermaid, the Drifter, and the Tea Shell

AHHH, SO THE tea cup has caught your fancy, eh? Well, I can't be sure, but I think this is one of the cups and saucers from the original Old Mermaids Tea Shell. You look confused. You've never heard me talk about it before, have you? This is the first piece I've found from the Old Mermaids Tea Shell, so I guess it's time to tell the tale.

The Old Mermaids built the Tea Shell on the edge of the Old Mermaid Sanctuary where they had made their homes since the Old Sea dried up and they washed up on the shores of the New Desert like moon-beautiful pieces of driftwood. It was a small place, the Old Mermaids Tea Shell, much like the Old Mermaids art and writing studio. It was big enough to hold an Old Mermaid or two, three or four small round tables with a couple of chairs each, and shelf after shelf of teapots, teacups, and bottles of tea. Sister Sophia Mermaid wanted a place where fellow travelers of the New Desert could sit for a spell, relax, and sip a bit of tea.

Now those of you who are familiar with the Old Mermaids know that Sister Sophia Mermaid was not the most likely Old Mermaid to decide to go into the hospitality business. She could be rather contrary. This may have been because she knew a great deal about a great many things. She took seriously the gnostic meaning of her name: Wisdom. And since she knew so much, she wanted to share her knowledge. She didn't want to preach. She didn't think she had all the answers. She just wanted to tell people what she knew, if they were interested, and argue—or discuss—the issue with them if they were wrong about something.

Sister Sophia Mermaid learned best when she was involved in a dialogue. What better way to start a conversation than by having a place where people could come to do just that? Sissy Maggie Mermaid painted sycamore trees in each corner of the Old Mermaids Tea Shell. Sister Sophia Mermaid also gave her a list of quotes, which Sissy Maggie stenciled on the walls. Some of them were Old Mermaid quotes. Others were little bits of wisdom Sister Sophia Mermaid had picked up over the years. "Never try to stop a wave." "Shallow water is for shallow people; deep water is for those who can swim." "A watched pot eventually boils." "The sun shines." "This is not the end of the world, it just feels like it." "At the beginning there was be."

Now understand this: The Old Mermaids used the word "tea" loosely. The Old Neighbor was the first to point this out to them. When they first opened the Old Mermaids Tea Shell, the

 The First Book of

Old Neighbor and the Old Neighbor's Husband were their first customers, only they didn't call them customers. They weren't buying anything. Sister Sophia Mermaid said, "We don't call visitors to our home 'customers.' This is part of our home, and travelers, friends, and neighbors can drift in and out."

"Then they shall be called drifters!" Sister Ruby Rosarita Mermaid said.

Sister Ruby Rosarita Mermaid and Sissy Maggie Mermaid were partners in this adventure of Sister Sophia Mermaid's. All the Old Mermaids supported Sister Sophia Mermaid's desire to open the Old Mermaids Tea Shell, but Sister Ruby Rosarita Mermaid offered to make desserts and soup for the drifters who came upon the Old Mermaids Tea Shell. Sister Sophia Mermaid thought that would be a grand thing. And Sissy Maggie Mermaid was an exceptionally hospitable Old Mermaid, and Sister Sophia Mermaid thought she would be a great asset to the Old Mermaids Tea Shell.

Anyway, I told you that the Old Neighbor and the Old Neighbor's Husband were the first drifters to the Old Mermaids Tea Shell. As always, the Old Neighbor had to see for herself what was happening in her part of the world. Sister Sophia Mermaid was glad she came. She knew the Old Neighbor would get the word out, and soon the Old Mermaids Tea Shell would be overflowing with drifters.

Sissy Maggie Mermaid and Sister Ruby Rosarita Mermaid had not finished writing out the menus—they kept drawing pictures next to each listing of a particular tea, so it was taking some time to complete it. Sister Sophia Mermaid stood by the table and listed out loud the variety of teas for the Old Neighbor and the Old Neighbor's Husband.

"But Sister Sophia Mermaid," the Old Neighbor said when she had finished, "you haven't listed teas at all. I'm not sure what they are. Perhaps you could call them tisanes. Maybe infusions. But none of them are teas. Teas are from the camellia sinensis plant."

"Old Neighbor, we can certainly make you tea from the camellia sinensis plant," Sister Sophia Mermaid said. "We have leaves gathered for us by the cloud wanderers themselves. But you are wrong to say that tea only comes from that plant. The language changes, and now tea can be a variety of drinks. Why not try the Essence of Coyote Laughter Tea? Or A Sip of Rattlesnake Moxie Tea. I bet you would enjoy Crackle of Thunder Tea."

Old Neighbor made a face for each tea Sister Sophia Mermaid mentioned, but Old Neighbor's Husband said he wanted to try the Wisdom of the Desert Faery Tea blended with a touch of the Cloud Dust and Sliver of Moonlight Teas, so the Old Neighbor agreed to black tea (Cloud Wanderer Tea) with a Hint of the Old Sea Tea.

Sissy Maggie Mermaid and Sister Ruby Rosarita Mermaid brought their neighbors tea along with a small basket of You're So Beautiful Biscuits. The three Old Mermaids watched as the couple sipped and stirred and chewed. Finally Old Neighbor leaned back, cocked an eyebrow, and said, "It was a good cup of tea, my dears. As usual, you don't disappoint. What do we owe you?"

"Owe us?" Sister Sophia Mermaid asked.

"What kind of compensation, dears?"

The Old Mermaids stared at her. The Old Neighbor rolled her eyes. "Sometimes I wonder about you Old Mermaids," she said. "It's as though you come from another country or something. We want to pay you for the tea and biscuits."

"Oh no," Sister Ruby Rosarita Mermaid said. "It's on the tea shell."

"What?"

"Isn't that an expression?" Sister Ruby Rosarita Mermaid said. "It's on the house? Since this is the Old Mermaids Tea Shell, then it's on the tea shell."

"Gratis," Sister Sophia Mermaid explained.

"Thank you," Old Neighbor said.

"I quite enjoyed the Wisdom of the Desert Faery Tea," Old Neighbor's Husband said. "I feel just a bit wiser myself right now. No desert faeries were harmed in the making of this tea, no doubt."

"No doubt!" Sissy Maggie Mermaid said. "Causing harm would not be the Old Mermaid way."

"We shall see you again," the Old Neighbor said.

And so it began. One by one, neighbors and strangers drifted into the Old Mermaids Tea Shell. Sometimes Sister Sophia Mermaid talked with the visitor for a bit and then recommended a particular tea. Ofttimes she seemed to know just what they needed. Soon the tea shell was overcrowded with teatotalers. The Old Mermaids set up tables and chairs outside the Tea Shell.

It was quite a thing to witness, all these people sitting around sipping X Marks the Spot Roadrunner Tea, Sassy Saguaro Tea, Magic of Hummingbird Tea, The Great Horned

Owl Hootin' and Hollerin' Tea, West Wind Whimsy Tea, A Spot of Prickly Pear Tea. You could see them contemplating the drink, observing their bodies and the immediate area for signs of a reaction to what they were drinking. Heads nodded and bobbed. "Yep, this does put me in mind of a hummingbird. I can definitely say that." "I just thought I heard an owl hootin'. You?" "I never thought of the West Wind as having whimsy. But I believe I was wrong about that."

At first, Sister Sophia Mermaid and the others went out into the desert collecting for the Old Mermaids Tea Shell. They went when the moon was brightest, or just before the sun came up, or midafternoon—you know, those betwixt and between times, the sleepy times when all manners of creatures wander through your world, this world, other worlds. And they would whisper to the Visibles and Invisibles and ask if they could have a bit of coyote song or desert faery magic or rabbit runnin' or cloud essence for their teas. They set out clear glass jars until they got an answer. Then they emptied the jars into cloth bags Sissy Maggie Mermaid, Sister Lyra Musica Mermaid, Sister Bridget Mermaid, and Sister Faye Mermaid had decorated and sang to and laughed over. Sister Sophia Mermaid carefully labeled each bag, then dropped the contents of them into the appropriate jars when she returned to the Old Mermaids Tea Shell.

After this first batch of teas was so successful, Sister Sophia Mermaid decided to try something new. She went out into the desert in search of joy, love, peace, goodwill, laughter, and acceptance. The others went with her. They didn't have far to go. They set the jars down next to themselves and danced joyfully, loved each other, felt at peace, extended goodwill to one another, laughed themselves silly, and accepted that they had done a good thing. They took the cloth bags back to the Tea Shell and put the contents of each into the appropriate jars and wrote new menus.

The new teas were a hit, naturally! On certain unspecified days, Sister Sophia Mermaid would put one of the teas on special.

She would write on the special board something like: "Two cups of Dances With Joy Tea for the price of none." Ah, you should have been there that day. People danced inside and all around the Tea Shell. Most people agreed that the Laugh Yourself Silly Tea Day was the most fun, although Love the One You're Always With Tea Day was a close second.

One hot summer day, a young woman drifted into the Old Mermaids Tea Shell. She was dusty and tired-looking and a stranger to the Old Mermaids.

"What is this place?" the young woman asked as she slapped her hat against her jeans. Dust rose from the hat and her pants.

"This is the Old Mermaids Tea Shell," Sissy Maggie Mermaid said. "Welcome. You look hot and thirsty. We have some Hint of Winter Tea on special today."

Betty, the Woman Who Weaves, and Louie, the Man Who Collects, were sitting at a nearby table.

"Yes, the Hint of Winter Tea is very refreshing," Betty said. "I would highly recommend it."

"My favorite is Coyote Wisdom Brew," he said. "It's a blend. My day doesn't feel quite right without it."

The young woman sat at an empty table. "I'll take something cold," she said. "Anything to eat?"

"We have Precious Prickly Pear soup," Sissy Maggie Mermaid said.

"That doesn't sound good," the young woman said.

"There's only the essence of prickly pear in it," Sister Ruby Rosarita Mermaid said. "It's a lovely vegetable soup."

"Then why do you call it prickly pear soup?"

"Precious Prickly Pear soup," Sister Ruby Rosarita Mermaid said. "Because the prickly pear essence gives it its oomph. And it thickens it up a bit."

Sister Sophia Mermaid was watching all this from the preparation area, her arms folded across her chest. She recognized a fellow contrarian when she saw one. She went over to the young woman's table, pulled out a chair, and sat with her.

"Who are you?" the girl asked.

"I am Sister Sophia Mermaid," she said. "I am very pleased to meet you."

"Sister?" the girl said. "Are you a religious sect?"

"No," Sister Sophia Mermaid said. "We washed up here some time ago, when the Old Sea dried up."

The girl looked over at Betty and Louie. "Do you know what she is talking about?"

"Oh yes," Betty, the Woman Who Weaves, said. "The Old Mermaids are very wise, especially Sister Sophia Mermaid.

"I don't really understand what they're talking about half the time," Louie, the Man Who Collects, said. "But it's fun listening to them."

"What do you like to be called?" Sister Sophia Mermaid asked.

"I don't like to be called anything," she said. "But people call me Gaby. It's from Gabriela."

Sissy Maggie Mermaid set down a glass of Hint of Winter Tea in front of Gaby. She picked it up and gulped the contents. She set the glass down hard when she was finished. "You forgot the tea part," she said, "but that cold water sure tasted good."

Sissy Maggie Mermaid shook her head. "No, it's there. This is sun tea. We put a bag of Hint of Winter Tea in it and then set it in the sun for a few hours. It's best when it's brewed for at least three hours. Then you really get the taste of winter in the mountains." Sissy Maggie Mermaid shivered as though cold. She grinned. "Isn't it great?"

Gaby said, "That was water, pure and simple. What are you people trying to sell me?"

"We're not selling you anything," Sister Sophia Mermaid said. "Here's your soup."

Sister Ruby Rosarita Mermaid served Gaby a steaming bowl of soup. The girl ate it quickly. Sister Sophia Mermaid wondered how long it had been since she had eaten. Sister Ruby Rosarita Mermaid kept refilling her bowl until she finally shook her head, indicating that she was full.

About then, Raul, the Man Who Cares for the Acequia, and Michael, the Man Who Finds Art, came into the Old Mermaids Tea Shell.

"We're here for our daily fix!" Raul said.

"Good afternoon, Old Mermaids and friends," Michael said as they sat at an empty table. "I'll have the usual."

"Night Stars Sizzle Tea," Sister Ruby Rosarita Mermaid said, "coming up."

"Um, let's see," Raul said, glancing at the special board and then down at the menu on the table. "I have been feeling a bit glum. It's so hot, you know. I could use a little Laugh Yourself Silly Tea. Sissy Maggie Mermaid, come flirt with me. Michael has been so cranky today."

Sissy Maggie Mermaid came and put her hands on Michael's shoulders. "Wait until he gets his tea," she said. "Then he'll be much better. Next week I hope to get some Essence of Man in the Arroyo Tea. That'll cheer you both up. I've seen this man wandering around at night, and he's gorgeous!"

"Sissy Maggie Mermaid," Sister Sophia Mermaid said, "that wasn't a man, it was a mountain lion."

"Oh, but what a mountain lion," she said, winking at Raul.

Everyone laughed. Except Gaby. Sissy Maggie Mermaid brought the men their tea, and they sipped their brews quietly.

Then Michael said, "Yes, I can feel the cool yet sizzling light of the night stars. A piquant brew."

Raul started laughing. When Gaby looked at him, he pointed to the cup. "You should try it," he said. "Laugh Yourself Silly Tea. It never fails."

Gaby got up and went to the men's table and looked into their cups.

"I don't see anything but water," she said. She looked into Betty and Louie's almost empty tea cups. "Nothing but water there, too. Are you people all nuts?"

"Why don't you give her some Wisdom of Desert Faery Tea?" Betty suggested.

"I don't want any Desert Faery Wiseass tea," Gaby said. "There ain't no such things as desert faeries. I don't even think there's any such thing as wisdom." She walked around the Tea Shell, reading the sayings on the wall. "Come on, what does this mean, 'a good bean is hard to find, everything else is easy?' Nothing else is easy! Have you all been out in the world? It's ugly. There are bad things happening. No amount of Pretend Life is Great tea is going to change that."

Sister Sophia Mermaid said, "No one is pretending anything. Come, try some more tea. Maybe there will be something to your taste."

Gaby looked around the Tea Shell and Sister Sophia Mermaid thought that she might break something, but just then Grand Mother Yemaya Mermaid and Sister Star Stupendous Mermaid came into the Tea Shell. Grand Mother Yemaya Mermaid smiled as she looked around. "Ahhh, old friends and new friends! Isn't it a great thing?" They went over and greeted Michael and Raul, then Louie and Betty. Gaby went back and sat at her table.

Grand Mother Yemaya Mermaid said to her, "Hello, little gypsy. Welcome to the Old Mermaid Sanctuary."

"Sanctuary?"

"Yes," Sister Star Stupendous Mermaid said. "Every wanderer can use some sanctuary now and again. You are welcome to it."

"The young woman believes we are all hiding from the reality of the world," Betty, the Woman Who Weaves, said.

Grand Mother Yemaya Mermaid nodded. "Yes, sometimes it is difficult to believe that this is a part of the world." She smiled. "But it is. We are going out to collect some essence of saguaro flowers. Ahhh, the wisdom of the saguaro. The stories they tell! The flowers know everything."

"And the trees know even more," Sister Star Stupendous Mermaid said, "so we'll stop by the Old Mesquite, too. Ta!"

The two Old Mermaids waved. Grand Mother Yemaya Mermaid winked at Gaby, then they left.

"What a breath of fresh air!" Betty said.

"Always," Louie agreed.

"That's a great idea for a tea," Sister Sophia Mermaid said, "Grand Mother Yemaya Mermaid's Breath of Fresh Air Tea."

Gaby shook her head. "I still think you're all nuts. You can't just sit here and do nothing while terrible things are going on outside."

"I remember when we first left the Old Sea," Sister Sophia Mermaid said. "We were all so sad. We felt like there was nothing we could do. We were lost, and we felt homeless. We missed the Old Sea. One day I happened to see a bobcat in the wash. She just stepped down into the sand and stared at me. Then she started walking away. She stopped and looked back at me as if to say, 'This way to the promised land.' Isn't that what we're all looking for?"

"Either that or the promised sea," Sister Ruby Rosarita Mermaid said.

"I followed the bobcat, staying at a bit of distance," Sister Sophia Mermaid said. "I kept waiting for things to change or be different, or for something to happen. But nothing did. We just walked the wash, both of us looking from side to side now and again. It was the same old wash. But after a while,

I started wondering what she saw. What was the wash like to her? I squatted down a bit, I tried to feel the ground through my shoes, I breathed the desert air deeply. I did this for a while. I wondered if the bobcat was imagining herself as me. Maybe, maybe not. But I began seeing the wash differently. I saw a cool spot under the palo verde, a great place to lounge out of the sun. And right there in that clear area, I could bask in the sun when it was cool. A rabbit hole. I could wait near and snatch me up a rabbit. I saw the wash as a bobcat saw the wash. And it was a different world. And the same. After a while, the bobcat went on her way, and I returned to the Old Mermaid Sanctuary and helped build our house."

"Is that story supposed to mean something to me?" Gaby asked.

"You want a different world, drifter," Sister Sophia Mermaid said, "and it's already different."

Sister Sophia Mermaid looked into the young woman's eyes. She had never seen anyone who appeared quite as sad as Miss Gabriela did. Sister Sophia Mermaid pushed away from the table and got up. "I think I have just the tea you need." She went to the preparation area, took a bag from a jar and dropped it into a pot of hot water Sister Ruby Rosarita Mermaid held out to her. She put the pot and a cup on a tea tray. It may have been this particular teacup, although I can't be sure. Sissy Maggie Mermaid added a small plate of You Are So Beautiful Biscuits, and Sister Sophia Mermaid carried the tray over to the table. She first set the cookies on the table off to the side. Then she put the empty cup and full pot in front of Gaby. Sissy Maggie Mermaid took away the tray.

Sister Sophia Mermaid tipped the pot and poured the tea into the cup.

"Let it sit for a few moments," Sister Sophia Mermaid said. "That really brings out the flavor. You know, you're right, Gabriela. There are many things going on in the world that are ugly and cruel and horrible. None of us here denies that. We each do what we can to bring beauty into the world. Go ahead, you can drink it now. We each do what we can to see beauty before us, behind us, beside us, above and below us, all around us. That is the Navaho prayer, that is the prayer of many people around the world."

Gaby lifted the cup and sipped the hot liquid.

"We have all felt homeless at one time or another," Sister Sophia Mermaid said. "As Grand Mother Yemaya Mermaid said, we could all use some sanctuary now and again."

Tears began falling down Gaby's cheeks.

"I am tired of wandering," Gaby said. "Tired of seeing it all. Why do I see it and others don't?"

"But that's who you are," Sister Sophia Mermaid said. "That's what you do."

Gaby nodded. The tears began flowing in earnest. The air in the Tea Shell changed, so that the other drifters looked at each other, wondering if it was going to rain. Was it time for the monsoons?

"You are seeing everything from tired eyes," Sister Sophia Mermaid said. "You need to see things through old eyes, through Old Mermaid eyes for a while. Then you'll figure out a way to articulate what you've seen and what you know."

Gaby nodded. Her tears fell into the teacup, and she drank

 The First Book of

them. When the pot was empty, Gaby's tears stopped.

"What kind of tea was that?" Gaby asked.

"What did it taste like?"

"Like the ocean," she said.

"That was Old Mermaid Tears Tea," Sister Sophia Mermaid said.

"Ooh," the other teatotalers said, nodding.

"You are very lucky," Michael said. "Old Mermaid Tears Tea is quite precious."

Gaby blinked and looked around the Old Mermaids Tea Shell. She smiled. "This is a wild place. I think I'd like to stay for a while. I could use the sanctuary. And the tea."

Sister Sophia Mermaid said, "You are welcome."

Gabriela stayed at the Old Mermaid Sanctuary for a time. She helped out at the Old Mermaids Tea Shell, and she became quite a connoisseur of tea and could explain the differences between each better than some of the Old Mermaids. Sister Sophia Mermaid especially enjoyed the vigorous discussions she and Gabriela continued to have throughout her stay. She encouraged Gabriela to write about her experiences, draw them, or teach people about what she knew.

When Gabriela was ready, she put back on her wandering shoes, as she said, and she prepared to leave the Old Mermaids. Sister Sophia Mermaid gave her several bags of tea from the Old Mermaids Tea Shell before she left.

"And you know how to make your own now," Sister Sophia Mermaid said.

"My own tears or my own teas?" Gabriela asked.

"Both," Sister Sophia Mermaid said. "Maybe one day we'll

see Old Mermaids Tea Shells all over the world, and we'll know you were there."

"I'll write you and let you know," she said.

The Old Mermaids covered Gabriela with kisses and hugs and gifts of all kinds and then watched as she drifted away. She stopped once and looked back at them. "This is a wild place!" she called. Then she kept walking.

The Old Mermaids wandered back to the Old Mermaids Tea Shell and had a pot of Gabriela's favorite blend of Old Mermaid Tears Tea, Wisdom of Desert Faery Tea, and Bobcat Wandering Tea. They cried a little, laughed a bit more, and told lots of stories about Gabriela and how she had drifted into their lives.

From the Old Mermaids Journal: No Coyotes Harmed

I LIKE THIS journal Annie gave you. She said she got the thread from Betty, the Woman Who Weaves, who got it out in the desert from Grandmother Spider. One day I hope Betty will let me tag along with her when she goes out to gather thread. I have heard it is an experience I will never forget. Or else I will forget it immediately. Grandmother Spider is like that. Who knows, maybe I've already gone out and harvested thread and forgotten. Whoa! Hadn't thought of that before.

Anyway, I wanted to thank you for the lovely day spent at the Old Mermaid Sanctuary. I know you've all said that thank yous are not needed because we all live in this desert together. But I remember Sister Faye Mermaid telling Tulip once that it was just polite to thank the wind, the sun, the water, the earth, the birds, the cacti—to thank all the elements of life, thank them for their gifts, to express our love for them. So that is what I am doing: thanking the elemental Old Mermaids for all your gifts.

Tulip has not had another nightmare since she met you. She is convinced now that every night she falls to sleep and grows two tails and swims in the Old Sea with all of you. Two tails like Grandmother Yemaya Mermaid used to have, she says, glittery, like the tiny pebbles in the wash. Blue-green like Sissy Maggie's eyes. Or Sister Sheila Na Giggles Mermaid's. Oops! I've forgotten. Ah well. Tulip remembers. (I'm talking a lot about forgetting and remembering, aren't I?)

Tulip remembers everything.

She remembers how the dirt in the wash feels on the soles of her feet.

She remembers the sound Old Crow makes when he laughs.

She remembers the kiss of the wind on her cheek.

She remembers to open her mouth when she gets butterflies in her tummy so they can fly out.

She remembers what the trail looks like after desert faeries have been there, so she can track them through the wash almost as well as the Old Man of the Mountains can track the mountain goats up the east ridge.

And she remembers to breathe, breathe, breathe it all in.

You taught her that. I am only her mother who was lost for so long. I'm finding my way now and I'm so grateful Tulip has had you all.

Did you hear her today at the Tea Shell? Billy Bad came in. You know how he kids around.

     The First Book of

"Hello, darlin'," he says to Sister Ruby Rosarita Mermaid. "I think I'll try that Coyote Whispers tea with the soup. I love your soup, Sister Ruby. And I've always wondered what those coyotes were whispering about. After I drink this tea, will I know? You didn't hurt any of them yippin' canines none to get at their whispers now, did you?"

Before Sister Ruby Rosarita Mermaid could say anything, before Sister Sheila Na Giggles Mermaid could slap Billy Bad on the back and ask him how he was doing and before he could say, "How do you think? Ain't I the picture of grandeur?" Before all that, Tulip said, "No coyotes were harmed in the making of this tea."

Billy Bad put his head back and laughed. Sounded more like a howl, actually. A coyote howl. I think Billy Bad has finally revealed himself to be what we always suspected he was: Our beloved trickster.

Tulip danced around the Tea Shell. Around Billy Bad, actually. He stood still in the middle of the floor holding Tulip's hand as she danced. Kind of seemed like he was dancing with her. Like the desert was suddenly incarnate in him. And Tulip was . . .Tulip was Tulip.

She's calling to me now. I better go. Be back soon.

See you in Tulip's dreams.

And maybe my own.

In love and gratitude,

Poppy

Tea Shell Offerings

Faery Dust Tea With A Hint of Agave Laughter

Lentil Storytelling Soup Soaked in Mountain Wisdom

In Love Apples & Blueberries Spilling With Secrets

Sister Lyra Musica Mermaid and the Recipe

S ISTER LYRA MUSICA Mermaid was certain she was more frightened than any of the other Old Mermaids. They all seemed to be adjusting to their new life away from the Old Sea more quickly than she was. She still clutched an old sea shell in her left hand—all of the time. Sometimes she held it to her ear in hopes of hearing the ocean or some sign that her old life had not completely disappeared. Once, a drop of water slipped out of the shell, like a teardrop, and Sister Lyra Musica Mermaid pressed it against her cheek with such longing that she dropped to the desert floor and added her own tears to the ocean teardrop. She licked her tears off of her lips while she sat on the hard ground and watched for scary little creatures who might bite her.

Sometimes she ached to hear water so much that she could hardly bear it. She would stand under the blue, blue sky and look for clouds. She would listen to the night to see if she could hear water calling to her from somewhere. She turned to the east and to the south and to the west and to the north. It was so quiet, except for the faint sound of her blood in her ears. Or was it the long lost Old Sea pleading with her to come home?

Sister Lyra Musica Mermaid felt a loneliness she had never known in the Old Sea. She had always felt in communion with everything in the Old Sea—she was constantly embraced, stroked, fed. The Old Sea was a being she knew in every cell of her body.

And now the Old Sea was gone. How could the knowledge of that loss not crush her? Not crush them all?

This day her sobs hiccoughed in her chest as the tears flowed down her face. She needed to be with the others. She picked herself up off of the ground and went to find her sister mermaids. They were gathering up dirt and animal dung and mixing it all with water to make bricks for the house they were creating.

Sister Sheila Na Giggles said to her. "I see you are making water. Good. We could use it. That is part of the recipe of this home-making material. Combine tears and earth. Then stir."

"And bake until done," Sister Ruby Rosarita Mermaid said.

The Old Mermaids laughed.

Sister Lyra Musica Mermaid looked up at the sun. "The baking part shouldn't be difficult."

Grand Mother Yemaya Mermaid rested her hand on Sister Lyra Musica Mermaid's shoulder for a moment; then she sat on the ground and began working the soil and water between

     The First Book of

her hands.

"With our breath, we combine earth, sun, and tears," Sister Faye Mermaid chanted. "Transforming our fears and tears into house and home."

"House and home," the others repeated. "House and home."

"I love the feel of this earth between my fingers," Sister Magdelene Mermaid said. "It feels so stable and flexible at the same time. And the color! It's sunlight in a brick. Only the Earth could make such color!"

"Oh, Sissy Maggie Mermaid, you love everything," Sister Bea Wilder Mermaid said. "Remember how you fell in love with the Moon when we first got here?"

"I don't see why you didn't all fall in love with the Moon," Sissy Maggie Mermaid said. "But now, I love this dirt, too. See what a little moisture will do to hard dirt? That's what this old world could use, a little Old Mermaid loving."

Sister Sophia Mermaid rolled her eyes. "You are wise beyond your years, Sissy Maggie Mermaid."

"Indeed she is," Mother Star Stupendous Mermaid said. "This dirt is quite lovely. And did you notice the color of the sky at night here? Something very dark and mysterious about it."

"We've seen the sky before—" Sister Ursula Divine Mermaid said. She hesitated and then added, "—before the Old Sea dried up."

"Yes, but not this sky," Mother Star Stupendous Mermaid said.

"I know what you mean," Sister Laughs A Lot Mermaid said. "It is different. The stars aren't brighter, but they shine differently. As though they are musical instruments and we can see them tremble each time they play a note, but we're too far away to hear what the song is."

"I remember when I was small, my parents told me that stars were really the teardrops of a giant," Sister DeeDee Lightful said. "She got lost up there and couldn't find her way home. She began to cry, but she was so far from home and so far from the Old Sea or any kind of sea that her tears had no place to go. Each one just floated up there in the sky, catching the moonlight at night and reflecting it back to here. Her people saw the star tear drops and followed them to find the lost giant and bring her back home. They left the tears up there to help others who were lost find their way back home."

The Old Mermaids looked up at the starless blue sky. The quiet pulsed around them.

"Maybe we should try that," Sister Lyra Musica Mermaid said.

"I tried," Sister DeeDee Lightful said. "I got lost in the desert."

"Yep, I looked for her for hours," Sister Bea Wilder Mermaid said.

"I never heard about that," Sister Lyra Musica Mermaid said.

"But I did find a waterfall," Sister DeeDee Lightful Mermaid said. "Or rather the Old Woman and the Old Man of the Mountains found it and showed it to us. It is so lovely. We should all go there."

"Yes, let's," Sister Bridget Mermaid said, "after we get part of the house done."

     The First Book of

"It has the most beautiful pool of water near it," Sister Bea Wilder Mermaid said. "We could make our own pool here that looks like it."

"I can't wait to paint the walls of this house," Sissy Maggie Mermaid said. "I've always longed to paint."

"Is there anything you don't long to do?" Sister Sophia Mermaid asked.

Sissy Maggie Mermaid shrugged. "I don't think so, but I'll let you know. I do love the feel of this dirt. You should try it, Sister Lyra Musica Mermaid."

Sister Lyra Musica Mermaid squatted between Sister Faye Mermaid and Grand Mother Yemaya Mermaid. She put her hands in the mixture. She couldn't help but smile.

"It tickles, doesn't it?" Sister Laughs A Lot Mermaid said. "We were talking about that. We missed you. Where were you?"

"I was in the wash," Sister Lyra Musica Mermaid said. "Feeling a bit lost."

"So you were crying?" Grand Mother Yemaya Mermaid said. "That is good. You remembered."

"Remembered what?" Sister Lyra Musica Mermaid asked. She kneaded the clay between her fingers. It felt like the bread dough she helped Sister Ruby Rosarita Mermaid make sometimes.

"Laugh or weep," Grand Mother Yemaya Mermaid said, "we swim in your tears."

"So we don't need to follow the star tears," Sister DeeDee Lightful Mermaid said. "We can just follow our own tears."

"Enough of this," Sister Sophia Mermaid said. "Let's figure

out our next meal. I'm not swimming in tears or anywhere else if I don't get some food."

"And this animal dung is getting a little stinky," Sister Laughs A Lot Mermaid said.

"Probably because we didn't get permission from the animals to use it," Sister DeeDee Lightful Mermaid said.

"We asked," Sister Ursula Divine Mermaid said. "They didn't care."

"Food!" Sister Sophia Mermaid said. "I must have food!"

"Now this feels just like home," Sissy Maggie Mermaid said.

"Yes, it does," Sister Lyra Musica Mermaid said. She licked her lips. No more tears right then, just sweat, and like her tears, they tasted like the Old Sea.

From the Old Mermaids Journal: Morsels

LAST NIGHT SISTER Ursula Divine Mermaid walked out into the desert and found the Moon fishing.

Coyote trotted by and warned, "Watch out. There's enough for everyone."

Sister Ursula Divine Mermaid walked deep into the desert to look for wild things. Road Runner ran by her.

"Can you tell if I am coming or going?" Road Runner asked.

"Does it matter?" she answered.

Road Runner chuckled. "Good answer."

Then he went away or came closer. Sister Ursula Divine Mermaid smiled.

It's always a good day when a Road Runner chuckles.

Sister Ruby Rosarita Mermaid and the Storytelling Soup

SISTER RUBY ROSARITA Mermaid adjusted to life in the New Desert after the Old Sea dried up more quickly than the other Old Mermaids. Of course she missed the Old Sea and all that was within. But she knew the Old Sea was in the clouds, her blood, and in every cell of the Old Salmon who made their way up and down various creeks and rivers. So it wasn't that she didn't love the Old Sea as much as the other Old Mermaids; it was that she loved the New Desert, too.

Sister Ruby Rosarita Mermaid appreciated the New Desert for exactly what it was: dry, sparse, mysterious, dangerous, beautiful. And in the New Desert she discovered her calling, her gift, the thing she loved to do almost more than anything else: Sister Ruby Rosarita Mermaid learned to cook.

She had never cooked in the Old Sea. No one had. It wasn't

done. Probably couldn't be done. But in the New Desert, Sister Ruby Rosarita Mermaid took to cooking like a fish takes to water. She went around to all the neighbors in the New Desert and up to the Mountains where the Old Man and Old Woman lived. She ate the meals they prepared for her, asked questions, then went out in the New Desert and discovered other things to eat. After she learned to cook, she taught the other Old Mermaids how.

All the Old Mermaids participated in their daily nourishment, but everyone knew that the meals created by Sister Ruby Rosarita Mermaid were special. Some of you have already heard about the chili she made when she accidentally used water from the Old Sea that Sister Bridget Mermaid had saved for them. People are still talking about that chili, how it lasted until everyone was fed, how people came from all over to eat at the Old Mermaid Sanctuary that day, how even the birds in the kitchen tile flew out and hovered around the soup pot to see what wondrous stew was brewing because it smelled so good—even to birds.

No one knew what would happen when Sister Ruby Rosarita Mermaid cooked, but they knew something would happen—especially when she made soup. Her dishes were always nutritious, of course; the ingredients were healthy, grown or plucked or harvested, all obtained with love and good nature. People said that when Sister Ruby Rosarita Mermaid made soup she whispered a little something extra into the pot, or maybe she added a special herb or some other ingredient. Most people didn't care what she did; they just knew they felt better after eating her food. Sometimes they felt happy; sometimes

     The First Book of

they began telling their secrets; sometimes they realized what their true heart's desire was; sometimes they understood the language of the cacti or the quail or the coyotes.

When people asked Sister Ruby Rosarita Mermaid why her food was so special, she'd say, "I discovered the best spice of all: happenstance." Then she'd laugh. Sister Ruby Rosarita Mermaid normally didn't get flustered or depressed or irritated. It just wasn't her nature. I don't mean she didn't have normal feelings. She did. She'd feel bad when something bad happened; she'd feel good when something good happened; then she moved on. She was interested in what was occurring right at that moment. She had to be, she'd say, otherwise she'd burn something.

Sister Ruby Rosarita Mermaid believed most problems between people could be solved by sitting around a meal together. The food connected them, became a part of them, and therefore they were connected to one another.

Then the Javelina Conflict erupted. It began when the Peppermans moved into the New Desert. They bought the house and land the Old Woman Who Talked to Cacti left behind after she followed the sun south. The neighbors all went to welcome the Peppermans. The Old Neighbor and the Old Neighbor's Husband brought them a rhubarb pie. Louie, the Man Who Collects, and Betty, the Woman Who Weaves, gave them a welcome mat for the front door that Betty had woven from things Louie found in the desert. The Old Man and Old Woman of the Mountains extended their welcome via a pleasant breeze that came out of the north.

The Old Mermaids brought the Peppermans a basket full

of wishes for their good health and long life, along with vegetables from the garden, art created by Sissy Maggie Mermaid and Sister Lyra Musica Mermaid, and an invitation to dine with them. The Peppermans weren't the friendliest couple, and the inhabitants of the New Desert didn't understand them much either. For one thing, the Peppermans seemed to have the same name. This confused everyone, so they decided to call them the Pepperman and the Pepperwoman. And no one was quite sure what they did. Of course, the Old Mermaids didn't care that they didn't do anything.

"But who are they?" the Old Neighbor asked.

"Who is any of us?" Sister Sophia Mermaid asked.

"No, really," the Old Neighbor said. "All of us do something. Louie collects. Betty weaves. Raul regulates the acequia. Vinetta organizes the markets—"

"Raul," Sissy Maggie Mermaid said. "Hmmm. I haven't seen him in a while. How is he doing?"

"And what do you do, Old Neighbor?" Sister Sophia Mermaid asked.

"She keeps track of what everyone is doing," Sister Faye Mermaid said. "Haven't you been paying attention?"

"So you must know everyone's stories then," Sister Bridget Mermaid said. "That is a good thing. We'd like to hear some of those stories."

"I will tell you this," Old Neighbor said. "There's going to be trouble."

"We were once new," Mother Star Stupendous Mermaid said. "You didn't know our stories. And now you are our friend."

 The First Book of

Old Neighbor shrugged.

"I bet you thought we'd be trouble, too," Sissy Maggie Mermaid said.

"Well, in your case I was right," Old Neighbor said.

The Old Mermaids laughed.

As the days turned into night and back into day, the Old Neighbor's prediction came true. The Pepperman and Pepperwoman did not like the javelinas who ran through the wash and up into the shrubbery around their house. The coyotes frightened them. And they did not want to hear anything about the mountain lions. They accused Louie, the Man Who Collects, and Betty, the Woman Who Weaves, of feeding the javelinas and thereby encouraging them.

Betty, the Woman Who Weaves, said she and Louie would never feed a wild animal, although they did put out seed or sugar water for the birds sometimes. Louie pointed out that the javelinas had been wandering the New Desert for a lot longer than any of them had been there.

"Perhaps if you talk with them," Louie said, "and explain that you'd rather they didn't dig near your house, they would stop coming around."

The Peppermans looked at him like he was a crazy man.

"And I suppose you want me to go out and howl with the coyotes and make friends with them, too?" Pepperman said.

"That's not a bad idea," Betty said.

The Peppermans asked Mr. Hunter to shoot the javelinas. Mr. Hunter said, "Are you going to eat them after I shoot them?"

"No!" the Pepperwoman said.

"Then I can't do it," Mr. Hunter said.

"You can eat them," the Pepperman said. "You can shoot and eat them all."

Mr. Hunter thought about this and then said, "I thank you for the offer, but I don't think so. The woman who calls me husband doesn't much like when I shoot our neighbors, even the hairy smelly ones."

"Then we're going to have to put up a fence," the Pepperman said.

"A fence?" Mr. Hunter shook his head. "You're lucky the woman who calls me husband doesn't like me to shoot our neighbors cuz she ain't gonna like this news."

Soon everyone had heard about the fence, and no one was happy. Many creatures wandered through the wash and the land that the Peppermans called their own. A fence would disrupt many lives.

Grand Mother Yemaya Mermaid and Mother Star Stupendous Mermaid visited the Pepperman and Pepperwoman and tried to find out what they could do to help them feel more comfortable.

"The desert is not a comfortable place," the Pepperwoman said. "And we must do what we can to protect ourselves and that which is ours."

"We certainly understand being new to a place," Mother Star Stupendous Mermaid said.

"Yes, indeed," Grand Mother Yemaya Mermaid said. "We came from a place very different from here."

"About as different as different can be," Mother Star Stupendous Mermaid said.

"Then you do understand," the Pepperwoman said. "You know we have to make this place our own. I need to make this place home."

"And javelinas can't be a part of your home?" Grand Mother Yemaya Mermaid asked.

"They stink and they're ugly!" the Pepperwoman said.

Grand Mother Yemaya Mermaid nodded. "We've all got something, don't we?"

Mother Star Stupendous said, "I understand that you don't feel at home here. That is our fault. We haven't made you feel welcome enough. You haven't heard our stories, and we haven't heard yours. Why don't you come to the Old Mermaid Sanctuary. We'll invite the entire neighborhood. Sister Ruby Rosarita Mermaid will make her famous storytelling soup, and we will tell stories. Afterward, if you still want to build a fence. We'll help you."

Grand Mother Yemaya Mermaid nodded.

The Pepperman and Pepperwoman glanced at one another. The Pepperman shrugged and the Pepperwoman said, "All right. Let us know what to bring. When would you like us to come?"

"Come when the day is shortest and the night is longest," Grand Mother Yemaya Mermaid said. "That is a great time for stories."

"And when is that?" the Pepperman asked.

The Old Mermaids did not look at each other in wonderment because this new man and woman did not know when the day was shortest and the night longest. Instead, Mother Star Stupendous Mermaid smiled and said, "Two days. Come for storytelling soup in two days."

And so Mother Star Stupendous Mermaid and Grand Mother Yemaya Mermaid returned to the Old Mermaid Sanctuary and told the others what had happened when they visited the Pepperman and Pepperwoman.

"Oh, that sounds wonderful," Sister DeeDee Lightful Mermaid said. "I must confess, though, that I don't recall Sister Ruby Rosarita Mermaid's famous storytelling soup."

"I don't remember it either," Sister Sheila Na Giggles Mermaid said.

"Nor I," Sister Faye Mermaid said.

Sister Ruby Rosarita Mermaid nodded. "I am beginning to remember it as though it is something I will create two days from now. I seem to recall that everyone who participates in the storytelling must bring an ingredient to add to the pot. All I do is boil the water, stir what drops into it, and sing a little chant. Our stories do the rest."

Mother Star Stupendous Mermaid nodded. "Just what we need."

Sister Lyra Musica Mermaid and Sister Laughs A Lot Mermaid volunteered to go out and invite all the neighbors to the storytelling feast. And so they did.

When the shortest day ended and the longest night began, Sister Ruby Rosarita Mermaid put on a pot of water to boil.

The Old Neighbor and the Old Neighbor's Husband were the first to arrive. The Old Neighbor brought pinto beans and dropped them into the pot.

"If this doesn't work," the Old Neighbor said, "everything will change."

                    The First Book of

"Everything is always changing," Sister Ruby Rosarita Mermaid said.

"But in this case, it isn't changing for the better," the Old Neighbor said. "And I don't see how this soup will help."

Sister Ruby Rosarita Mermaid stirred the beans and the water and sang one of her favorite chants to the becoming soup, "Beans, beans, we're Mermaid Queens. Make this stew a healing brew."

Louie, the Man Who Collects, and Betty, the Woman Who Weaves, came next. They brought pieces of chopped squash.

"Don't be nervous," Louie told Sister Ruby Rosarita Mermaid. "Don't give it a thought that the cohesiveness of our entire world depends upon this night and your soup."

Sister Ruby Rosarita Mermaid laughed. "No, I won't give it a thought." She stirred in the new ingredients. "Squash, squash, you fabulous nosh. Make this stew a healing brew."

Raul, the Man Who Cares for the Acequia, and Michael, the Man Who Finds Art, brought carrots. "Nice to see you both," she said as Michael dumped the carrots into the pot.

"I hope this will do the trick," Michael said. "All of us are depending upon your famous storytelling soup."

Sister Ruby Rosarita Mermaid kept stirring. She did not tell them this was the first time she had ever made storytelling soup because she knew something could be real and meaningful before it ever existed. "Carrots, carrots, with all your fine merits, help make this stew a healing brew."

Mr. Hunter and the Woman Who Calls Him Husband contributed chili peppers to the soup. Tulip and Poppy helped chop up the tomatoes they brought. Well, Tulip watched while her mother Poppy chopped. Someone else brought black beans. Someone else celery. When almost everyone had arrived except the Pepperman and Pepperwoman, the story goes that each of the Old Mermaids added something to the storytelling soup. Some say Mother Star Stupendous Mermaid sprinkled in star dust, but maybe it was only cumin. Sister Sheila Na Giggles dropped in a piece of trickery from the coyotes, or maybe it was a prickly pear pad. Sister DeeDee Lightful added some kind of spice, maybe it was cayenne, maybe it was the answer to all your questions.

Sister Ursula Divine Mermaid added minced bear wisdom, or it could have been garlic. It's sometimes hard to tell the difference. Sister Lyra Musica Mermaid and Sister Laughs A Lot Mermaid added sea salt Sister Bridget Mermaid had saved from the Old Sea. Everyone who was there and quite a few people who weren't said they could hear the waves of the ocean for a few minutes after the Old Mermaids salted the soup. Sister Sophia Mermaid added sea spray, or more salt and water. Grand Mother Yemaya Mermaid added moonlight. Sister Bea Wilder Mermaid dropped in a bird song she had heard from Annie, the Woman Who Loves Birds. And Sister Faye Mermaid shook in mystery, an important ingredient for any kind of magic or nourishment.

And still, the guests of honor had not arrived. Sister Ruby Rosarita Mermaid tasted the soup and shook her head. Something was missing.

Just before the grumbling would have started, the Pepperman and Pepperwoman arrived at the Old Mermaid Sanctuary. The Old Mermaids greeted them warmly. The other neighbors were a bit more restrained. They had visions of fences dancing in their heads. The Pepperman and Pepperwoman went into the kitchen. The Pepperwoman took out a bag and held it out to Sister Ruby Rosarita Mermaid.

"We come from a place where there is water," the Pepperwoman said. "And plants grow in this sea. They are deep dark green, and they undulate in the water. Our people dive into the water and cut these plants. We have many stories about them. Some believe they are strands of hair belonging to a great sea goddess. Some believe they are the lovely green locks of the mermaids who live in great cities below. In any case, we always ask permission before we cut their hair." She opened the bag and brought out pieces of dried seaweed.

"Oh!" Sister Ruby Rosarita Mermaid cried. "Sea vegetables!"

The other Old Mermaids gathered around to look at the seaweed. They grew quiet. A tear or two from the Old Mermaids may have dropped into the soup then as they remembered the Old Sea. It had been a very long time since they had had vegetables from the Old Sea.

"Go ahead," Sister Ruby Rosarita Mermaid said, and the Pepperwoman dropped pieces of the seaweed into the pot. Sister Ruby Rosarita Mermaid stirred the soup.

"Seaweed, seaweed, fill our needs. From the sea, from the sea, let it be, let it be, blessed sea."

Sister Ruby Rosarita Mermaid tasted the soup. "Yes, that was just what the soup needed. Thank you!"

The Pepperman and Pepperwoman looked at one another and smiled.

While the soup continued to bubble quietly, everyone gathered round and told stories. Sister Bea Wilder Mermaid talked about Annie, the Woman Who Loves Birds. Louie told a story about the time he and the coyotes had a singing contest during one of the full moons. At least he thought it was a contest. Betty said they were just yelling at him to shut-up so they could hear what the Moon was saying. Betty told the story of the quilt made from pieces of the desert. Sister Ursula Divine Mermaid talked about the journey she took up the mountain when she got a new name from the Bear and the Sycamore. Sister Lyra Musica Mermaid recalled the time Mr. Hunter almost hit her with an arrow because he kept mistaking Old Mermaids for deer and mountain lions. And speaking of mountain lions, Raul said, remember the old one-eyed lion who wandered the wash for years. He's retired now, Michael said; he's got a place down south with Old Woman Who Talked to Cacti. Everyone laughed at that, and more stories poured out about this or that place, this or that hill, this or that bend in the wash, this or that spring, summer, fall, or winter, this or that full or new moon.

Soon they were eating Sister Ruby Rosarita Mermaid's storytelling soup. They all agreed it was the best she had ever made, the best they had ever tasted.

"I only stirred the pot; you all brought the ingredients," Sister Ruby Rosarita Mermaid told them. "I just remembered something about the place where Old Woman Who Talked to Cacti used to live, the place where the Peppermans now live. The Old Woman talked to the cactus plants, yes, but you know, she talked to just about everything. A lot of us do that here in the New Desert. I talk to my food. I talk to every ingredient. I

     The First Book of

converse with them. I try to listen to what they say, too. Well, Old Woman Who Talked to Cacti had a soft spot for this hard desert, and she welcomed all the creatures who lived on her land or wandered through it. You wouldn't believe what she welcomed and who she talked to. She welcomed mice, rattle-snakes, black widow spiders, scorpions, coyotes, mountain lions. She liked the company. She liked any kind of company. She was able to get used to any kind of being, it seemed." Sister Ruby Rosarita Mermaid looked around at the gathering. "Don't you think that's true?"

The others nodded.

"Oh yeah," Michael said. "And she never killed anything. I remember sitting in her kitchen and there was a black widow spider up in the window. When I pointed it out to her, she said, 'Yes, she came by to have tea with you.' I said, 'Well I don't want to have tea with her!' She said, 'Keep your voice down. Black widow spiders are notoriously thin-skinned.' So I whispered, 'I don't want to have tea with her!'" He laughed. "I'm whispering so I don't hurt the spider's feelings. And I sat there and had tea with the Old Woman—and the black widow spider."

"Yep, that one-eyed mountain lion lived at her place for the longest time," Mr. Hunter said, "and she warned me not to harm a hair on its head. I asked if I could harm some hairs somewhere else on his body, but she didn't like that idea either."

They all laughed.

"She did have a lot more javelinas at her place than most of us," Betty said.

Sister Ruby Rosarita Mermaid nodded. "I asked her about

that once as we sat outside sipping some cold drink while we sucked up the musky scent of the javelinas who were digging around in her yard. I told her that the javelinas seemed especially fond of her. She said when she first came to the New Desert the javelinas were the first people to come say hello to her. She didn't recognize their greeting at first, she said. She was afraid of everything then, including the javelinas who kept digging up the ground, snorting at her, and waking her up at night with their strange sounds, stinking up the place.

"Even so, she started looking forward to their nocturnal visits. She'd sit out on the porch and wait for them. One night she finally said hello and told them they were welcome. One of them said 'thank you very much but we've been here forever and we were saying welcome to you. Humans usually tear up the earth and stink up a place, and we figure you all do that because you don't really understand what being home means, you don't really feel welcome wherever you go, so we're welcoming you, in the hopes that you'll feel like this is home—and you won't ruin it for the rest of us.' She was quite touched by this, so she thanked the javelinas. That was the beginning of her welcoming all kinds of creatures into her home, big and small, stinky and not so stinky."

"Yes," Mother Star Stupendous Mermaid said. "I had forgotten that story. Thanks for telling it, Sister Ruby Rosarita Mermaid."

The Pepperwoman and Pepperman were silent for the longest time. Then the Pepperwoman said, "Maybe the javelinas have been trying to welcome us to our new home."

"Maybe so," Sister Star Stupendous Mermaid said. "Now,

The First Book of

tell us stories of your home."

Everyone sat still, waiting for tales from the place where the Peppermans lived before coming to the New Desert.

The Pepperwoman hesitated and then said, "Well, it's just up the wash a ways from here. It's where the Old Woman Who Talked to Cacti used to live with the one-eyed mountain lion and the black widow spider who liked to come to tea. It's where the javelinas bring their kin to show them the man and the woman who welcome all."

Everyone there cheered and clapped. This was the welcome the Peppermans had always wanted and needed.

They all told more stories and ate more soup. People say the stories went on for hours, days, weeks, months until the longest night of the year ended. In the morning, the Old Mermaids and their neighbors welcomed the sun. The Woman and the Man Who Welcomed All thanked the Old Mermaids and then walked home alongside Louie, the Man Who Collects, and Betty, the Woman Who Weaves.

The Old Mermaids went back into the kitchen and finished off the last of the storytelling soup.

The Woman and the Man Who Welcomed All never built a fence. And every year on the longest night, Sister Ruby Rosarita Mermaid, the Old Mermaids, and all their neighbors made the famous storytelling soup together and told stories to each other until the sun came up.

Blessed sea.

From the Old Mermaids Journal: Siren Song

EVERYONE HAS A siren song. . . . It's whatever you do that you love completely. Something fluid, beautiful, all yours.

—*Myla Alvarez*, Church of the Old Mermaids

Sister Ursula Divine Mermaid and the Old Sycamore

I FEEL LIKE an Old Mermaid this morning right after they washed up onto shore. Right after the Old Sea dried up and they were left without their watery home. Stranded in the desert, drops of the Old Sea beading off of them like sweat. Their bodies changing, shapeshifting before their very eyes. Before the very eyes of the desert and the creatures come to gather at the old shoreline, some of them adrift, too, stranded in this New World. The Old Mermaids didn't huddle together in fear, however. They drifted up out of the wash, they moved up out of the wash, they strode up out of the wash as soon as they were able. They listened to the whispers of the desert. To the Earth that stroked their soles, saying, "It'll be, it'll be, it'll be." Then they built their house, their home, their lives.

One of the Old Mermaids had problems sleeping, however.

She had a little more trouble with the shifting of their lives than some of the others; although truth be told, they all had some difficulties. Sister Lyra Musica Mermaid was a bit afraid of the desert creatures for a while. Sister Laughs A Lot had nightmares. Grand Mother Yemaya Mermaid started snoring. And Sister Diana Mermaid couldn't sleep.

Sister Diana Mermaid who loved the Old Wild Things missed the creatures of the Old Sea. And she missed her Old Self. She was a tough Old Mermaid. Fit in mind and body. Yet while the other Old Mermaids got their land legs, Sister Diana Mermaid still felt watery. Sleepy. And that doesn't really work in a desert. She didn't tell anyone this, but she felt as if she had lost herself when the Old Sea dried up. Some nights she would try to fall to sleep by singing to herself, "My body lies over the ocean, my body lies over the sea, my body lies over the ocean, so bring back my body to me, to me." This was not her true siren song, however, and she still could not sleep.

One morning she watched the sun come up over the mountains, ending one more sleepless night. On this morning she heard the whisper of the mountain. Or maybe it was the whisper of the trees on the mountain. The Old Man and Old Woman of the Mountains talking in their sleep? She wasn't sure. She asked the other Old Mermaids if they could tell what the whisperer was saying. Every one of them told her they couldn't hear a thing.

"You know what this means then?" Mother Star Stupendous said.

Sister Diana Mermaid shook her head.

"It means the whisper is meant only for you," Grand Mother

   The First Book of

Yemaya said. "You must follow it to its source."

So Sister Ruby Rosarita Mermaid packed Sister Diana Mermaid a lunch, Sister Bridget Mermaid and Sister Faye Mermaid sang her a blessing, and the others wished her well— and off she went.

We can't be sure of exactly what happened. We've heard rumors. Some say she was up that mountain in a couple of hours. Some say she wandered for days, even months, while she had one exciting encounter after another. Some say she was so sleepy that she was lucky she did not fall into harm's way. My guess is she went up that Old Mountain in her own sweet time, stopping to talk with the Wild Things on her way up. She listened to their problems, offered suggestions, then went on her way again. She probably dropped in on the Old Man and the Old Woman of the Mountains. Or they dropped in to see her. And always she heard this whispering. She asked the Wild Things if they heard it. She asked the Old Woman and the Old Man if they heard it. They all said they did not hear it. "It is for you only, Sister Diana Mermaid."

Sister Diana Mermaid continued to wander, looking for the source of the whispering. She realized it was the whispering which had kept her awake these many nights. If she listened carefully, she thought it could almost be the sound the Old Sea made as it stroked the Earth, the sound it made when it came to shore and then went back out again. But it was more than that, and it was less comforting. It was more or less the Old Sea.

Then she was up above an old creekbed when she put out her hand to steady herself—she had not slept now in many many days and she was quite lost—and her hand touched bark.

She felt a spark of electricity, although she would not have called it that. She felt a spark. Period. A snippet of lightning. Heat. It went down to her toes. Just for a moment, and then it was gone. This beautiful tree had many branches that were like trunks and the bark had beautiful patterns—mottled, like a snake skin. It looked as though the tree shed its skin again and again to create a beautiful barkscape. Sister Diana Mermaid fell to her knees in admiration.

"You are the most beautiful tree I have ever seen," she said. "May I rest here for a while? I am looking for the source of the whispering that has been keeping me awake. Not awake awake. Just not sleeping." By way of answer, the Old Sycamore let drop a few of its nearly-star shaped leaves into Sister Diana Mermaid's lap. The Old Mermaid rested her back against the tree. "Perhaps I will just rest my eyes for a moment."

Right there and then Sister Diana Mermaid fell to sleep. When she opened her eyes, it was dark outside. And the Wild Things sat in a horseshoe around a nonexistent fire waiting for her. She squinted. Wait. There was a tiny flame where the non-existent fire wasn't. Flickering blue and red above the ground. Across from it, across from her, sat a big black creature.

"Is it you who has been whispering to me?" she asked.

"I do not whisper," the Old Black Being growled. "You have called to us, and we have come."

"But you are not the source of the whispering?"

The Old Black Being that was a Bear said, "We are not."

Sister Diana Mermaid sighed. "I have not told my sister mermaids this, but I miss our old life. I miss my old self. Now I am lost."

"We can help you with that," the Old Black Bear said. "We can tell you where you are."

"Where am I?" she asked.

"You are here," the Old Black Bear said.

Sister Diana Mermaid thought about this, and then she nodded. What the Old Black Bear said made perfect sense. Exquisite beautiful sense. She felt the Old Sycamore behind her supporting her. She felt the Earth beneath her. She felt the twinkle of the stars above her. She felt the presence of the Old and New Wild Things all around. She felt completely at home with herself, and she felt herself completely at home. She felt, she felt, she felt. Ahhhhh.

And then she heard the whispering again. This time she recognized it. It was the whispering of her own being. It was the whisper of the Old Sea pulsing inside her—pulsing inside every living being.

Sister Diana Mermaid gazed at the tiny flame in the non-existent fire.

"Does that belong to me?" she asked. She got up and walked to the tiny flame. The Old Black Bear took the flame onto her paw as she stood. It danced on her palm. She held it up to Sister Diana Mermaid's chest and then pressed it into her heart. It tickled, and Sister Diana Mermaid smiled. She felt warm. The warmth spread throughout her whole body. She shook herself until it all felt all right.

The Old and New Wild things cheered. Or roared. Growled. Howled.

"Welcome, Sister Ursula Divine Mermaid," the Old Black Bear said.

And that is how Sister Diana Mermaid became Sister Ursula Divine Mermaid. She Who Is Most At Home Where the Wild Things Live: in her own heart. They danced until dawn.

She opened her eyes, and it was morning. She wondered for a moment if it had all been a dream, but she knew it didn't matter. Old Mermaid dreams are very powerful indeed.

She hugged and thanked the Old Sycamore. She found a stick up against the tree, just her size. When she touched it, she felt the spark again. It flowed through her whole body, constantly—just like the Old Sea. She thanked the Old Sycamore for the walking stick. She looked around and knew right where she was.

She walked down the mountain and returned to the Old Mermaid Sanctuary where the Old Mermaids met her with wet kisses and Old Mermaid hugs.

 The First Book of

From the Old Mermaids Journal: Beelief

ONE DAY AS the Old Mermaids were walking back to the Old Mermaid Sanctuary after a visit with the Old Woman and Old Man of the Mountains, soon after the Old Mermaids had washed up on the shores of the New Desert, when they hadn't quite found their land legs and were not certain how to make their way in this New World, a swarm of bees came out of the woods or the desert or down from the sky or up from the earth, and they swirled around the Old Mermaids who stopped and listened. They had never heard anything quite like these bees. Was it the song of a thousand bees, a chant, a mantra, a hymn?

"I've heard it said that you can ask the wild bees what the druid knows," Sister Lyra Musica Mermaid whispered as the bees hummed all around them.

"Then we'll just hear back what *we* told the druids," Sister Bea Wilder Mermaid said.

The Old Mermaids chuckled in time to the beebop.

"What do you know, dearest bees?" Sister Ursula Divine Mermaid asked.

The Old Mermaids listened as the Old Bees answered.

A few moments later, the bees spiraled away from them, becoming a swirl of black and gold against the blue, blue sky.

Sister Ruby Rosarita Mermaid saw a drop of gold on her palm. She licked her hand. She tasted her skin and sweat and something so marvelous she didn't quite know what to say.

"Oh my," she finally whispered. "The Old Bees left us a gift."

The other Old Mermaids likewise found drops of gold on their palms and tasted it.

"It tastes like magic," Sister Laughs A Lot Mermaid said.

"Music," Sister Bridget Mermaid said. "I feel music."

"Look, I see a bit of sky in the gold," Sister Sophia Mermaid said.

"Laughter," said DeeDee Lightful Mermaid.

"Love," Sister Magdelene Mermaid said.

"Mmmm," Sister Faye Mermaid said. "A bit like ecstasy."

"Tastes like honey," Mother Star Stupendous Mermaid said, "which is all those things and more."

"Honey?" Sister Sheila Na Giggles said. "I thought honey was a myth. I guess I'm a believer now."

"The Old Bees always believed in us," Grand Mother Yemaya Mermaid said.

"What did you hear them say?" Sister Lyra Musica

   The First Book of

Mermaid asked.

Grand Mother Yemaya Mermaid smiled and put her arm across Sister Lyra Musica Mermaid's shoulders.

"The same thing you heard, sister," Grand Mother Yemaya Mermaid said.

"Beelieve," Sister Lyra Musica Mermaid said.

The other Old Mermaids nodded, and after a bit, they continued on their way, back toward the Old Mermaid Sanctuary, softly humming the new song from the Old Bees.

"Beelieve, beelieve, beelieve!"

Old Mermaids Elixir

Myla has set up her table—the Church of the Old Mermaids—in front of Antigone Books in Tucson on another Saturday. A woman walks over and picks up a clear glass bottle...

"What is this?" the woman asked. Lily leaned against Myla and watched the woman.

"Well, I can't be sure," Myla said, "but I believe that is the bottle that once contained the Old Mermaids Elixir, only it wasn't called that at first. A traveling salesman stopped by the Old Mermaid Sanctuary for a time. He had a big old colorful wagon drawn by two old horses. One was black, the other was white. The black one had a white spot on her forehead. The white one had a black spot on his forehead. The Old Mermaid Sanctuary neighbors came from all around to meet the horses and the salesman. His name was Grandy, I believe, and the horses were Black Beauty and White Wonder. You figure out which was which."

Lily giggled.

"Anyway, Grandy had all kinds of things to sell," Myla

said. "Grandy was just as you would imagine. He'd stand by his wagon and call out, 'Hear ye, hear ye! I've got what you need! I can heal your wounds, soothe your soul, fill your wallet—all without emptying it first.'

"The Old Mermaids appreciated his showmanship, and they let him stay at the Old Mermaid Sanctuary. They liked watching him because it was like going to a show, but they didn't buy anything from him. He told everyone exactly what was in each of his bottles, so they could decide whether what he was saying was true or not. But Sister Faye Mermaid and Sister Bridget Mermaid knew how to create their own concoctions and weave their own enchantments, and they thought most of what he was selling was sugar water. They kept an eye on him to make certain he wasn't causing any harm to their neighbors. They liked listening to his stories, and he enjoyed eating their food and watching Sissy Maggie Mermaid walk around half-dressed the way she did.

"Just before he packed up to leave, he told the Old Mermaids he had a present for them. 'It was given to me by an Old Merman sitting on the edge of the Old Sea,' Grandy said. He held out a clear glass bottle filled with liquid. 'He told me that one day I would know who it was for. He said it would help them find their tails again, so they could come home. I didn't know what he was talking about then, but I'm thinking maybe he was talking about you all.'

"Grand Mother Yemaya Mermaid took the bottle from him. On the label a mermaid swam alongside the words 'Mermaid Elixir.' In tiny letters below that it read 'Put one drop in your bathtub as needed.'

"Grand Mother Yemaya Mermaid said, 'The Old Merman put this label on here?'

"Grandy smiled. 'No, Grand Mother,' he said. 'I wrote up what he told me. I don't know what will happen when you use it, but it is yours to try and see.'

"Then Grandy made his farewells. The Old Mermaids hugged and kissed Black Beauty and White Wonder goodbye, and the wagon pulled away and soon disappeared in the dust. The Old Mermaids stood around looking at the bottle. They passed it from hand to hand, from Old Mermaid to Old Mermaid. Finally they opened it and smelled it. They did everything but drink it.

"'It can't be real,' Sister Bea Wilder Mermaid said. 'Why not?' Sister Laughs A Lot Mermaid asked. 'Because an Old Merman isn't going to give Grandy something like that,' Sister Ursula Divine Mermaid said. 'And I never heard of such a thing when we were in the Old Sea,' Sister Bridget Mermaid said. 'These are new times,' Sister Lyra Musica Mermaid said. 'And we didn't need it when we were in the Old Sea.'

"Sister DeeDee Lightful Mermaid said, 'Maybe this is providence. Maybe the Invisibles are trying to help us get back home.' The Old Mermaids looked around at each other. Mother Star Stupendous Mermaid said, 'We are home, Sister Mermaids. The Old Sea is gone, at least the Old Sea as we knew it. What would we do if we went back to the way we were? There is no place here for us as we were.'

"The Old Mermaids stood quietly under the summer sun and thought about what Mother Star Stupendous Mermaid said. Finally, Sister Sophia Mermaid said, 'What Mother Star

Stupendous Mermaid has told us is very wise. We should listen to her.'

"The other Old Mermaids agreed, although Sister DeeDee Lightful Mermaid hesitated. Even though they had been in the New Desert for some time, Sister DeeDee still felt as though she hadn't quite gotten her land legs. The other Old Mermaids went about their days, and Sister DeeDee Lightful Mermaid held onto the Mermaid Elixir for a while. Every once in a while she'd take off the top and dab a drop of it on her wrists. Nothing happened, but she kept doing it anyway. She would close her eyes and remember what it had been like in the Old Sea.

"One hot day when the Old Mermaids sought refuge from the sun and heat in the pool, Sister DeeDee Lightful Mermaid sat on the edge of the pool with her legs in the water; the open bottle of the Mermaid Elixir was next to her. Most of the other Old Mermaids swam or floated in the water. Sister Bea Wilder Mermaid came up behind Sister DeeDee Lightful Mermaid and tickled her until she fell into the water. Then Sister Bea Wilder Mermaid slipped into the water. She didn't see the Mermaid Elixir, and you can guess what happened. The entire bottle fell into the pool when Sister Bea accidentally knocked it over. Sister DeeDee Lightful Mermaid shrieked. The other Old Mermaids got very quiet. Sister Faye Mermaid said, 'Don't worry. The elixirs of a charlatan rarely work.'

"But something happened that day as this bottle you're holding—at least I think it was this bottle—fell into the pool and its contents mixed with the water in the pool. The Old Mermaids felt a kind of moisture in their beings that they

                    The First Book of

had not felt since they left the Old Sea. I can't be sure, but the story goes that all the tails of the Old Mermaids became visible again, and the Old Mermaids were creatures of the water again for a time. The sun glinted off the blue, green, red, yellow, black, scarlet, orange, indigo scales of the tails of the Old Mermaids. It wasn't that they went back to what they were exactly. It was more like they recognized that they were still themselves whether they were in the water or the desert. The Old Mermaids were able to swim in the knowledge of their true selves in that pool all day long. And it was a long day that lasted a week, a month, a year, a hundred years.

"Before they got out of the pool that long day, Sister DeeDee Lightful Mermaid swam to the bottom and picked up the Mermaid Elixir bottle which was now filled with pool water or mermaid elixir or both. Some say that the Old Mermaids never had to use the Mermaid Elixir again; whenever they jumped into the pool they became their old selves again. But Sister DeeDee Lightful Mermaid knew others might need help in recognizing their true selves, in finding their own tails—and tales—so she bottled the Old Mermaids Elixir and gave it out to friends and neighbors. She used the bottle of watered-down elixir as the Mother so she'd put a drop or more of the elixir into a bottle of water, put a label on it, and call it the Old Mermaids Elixir.

"Of course, she tried it out before she gave it to anyone. She was no charlatan. Everyone who used it said they saw themselves as they truly were, for good or ill. This truth never came as a surprise to anyone—or maybe it did. But they shouldn't have been surprised: Sister DeeDee Lightful

Mermaid had printed right on the label 'know thyself.'

"Time went on and as you know, the Old Mermaids had to leave the Old Mermaid Sanctuary. The story goes that whoever found the original Old Mermaids Elixir bottle could fill it up with ordinary water and it would become a true Old Mermaids Elixir. If you put a couple drops in your bath or in your pool or in your tea, you grow your own mermaid tails, or maybe you'll just discover your true self. Either way it'll be an adventure. You willing to try it? I can almost see your tail now, if I squint. Yep. You'll be swimming in the deep ocean of your true self any minute now."

—from An Old Mermaid Sanctuary

Sister Bea Wilder Mermaid and the Carved Bird

VISITORS TO THE Old Mermaid Sanctuary often did not recall Sister Bea Wilder Mermaid. It wasn't because she wasn't memorable. It was more that she was like the Old One-eyed Mountain Lion who wandered the wash that ran through the Old Mermaid Sanctuary: you didn't see him unless he wanted to be seen; otherwise, you could be looking right at him and you'd think you were seeing the blond desert floor.

Sister Bea Wilder Mermaid was not the most social of the Old Mermaids, and she was not always comfortable in groups. She was not unkind—no Old Mermaid was unkind—but she did seem a bit cross sometimes to those who didn't know her. She didn't understand the social niceties people engaged in here in the New Desert. While the other Old Mermaids learned to talk about the weather with visitors to the Old Mermaid Sanctuary,

Sister Bea Wilder Mermaid wondered how people could talk so much about something they had no control over.

Mother Star Stupendous Mermaid told her, "When they speak of the weather, it's like they're singing a chant they only half remember. No doubt their ancestors talked to the wind and rain and clouds—they'd sing to them—trying to negotiate good weather for their lives. It's how we talked to the Old Sea, only we remembered how and they've forgotten."

"Then perhaps we should have Sister Faye Mermaid teach them a sea chanty or two," Sister Bea Wilder Mermaid said.

"It is not their way," Grand Mother Yemaya Mermaid reminded her.

Despite any ideas about Sister Bea Wilder Mermaid's social skills, everyone from far and near knew that she could be counted on in a pinch. Even when nothing was pinching, actually. When the Old Mermaids first washed up on the shores of this particular desert, it was Sister Bea Wilder Mermaid who walked the wash and the surrounding area finding the lay of the land—quite different from finding the flow of the Old Sea. And Sister Bea Wilder Mermaid had known the flow of the Old Sea better than anyone else. She knew the shape of the curves and cliffs and gullies that the Old Sea filled with Her body. Sister Bea Wilder Mermaid knew she could leap from those cliffs and never be harmed. But here in this New Desert, that kind of easiness was no longer possible. This world was a prickly one.

It was Sister Bea Wilder Mermaid who first found the Old Woman and the Old Man of the Mountains soon after the Old Mermaids arrived in the New Desert. The Old Woman and the

Old Man listened to her tale of the Old Sea drying up. Then they stood on the land behind their house and they began whispering to the mountain and the desert below. Their hands made shapes in the air while they let the New Desert and its inhabitants know that the Old Mermaids were in the wash in the toes of the foothills of the mountain. "Give them succor. Afford them peace." The breath of the Old Woman and Old Man on Sister Bea Wilder Mermaid's face felt like a welcoming breeze. She returned to the Old Mermaids, who were carefully cleaning a space on the land for their new home, and brought them news of the land—including where an Old Stream wound through the desert, slowly, surely, so that all could dip in their cups and take a sip.

Sister Bea Wilder Mermaid understood that the Old Mermaids needed to learn the rhythms of their new world. Sister Faye Mermaid and Sister Bridget Mermaid conversed with the Invisibles of the place—they created new sea chanties and poems for their new home. They learned about the flora while Sister Ursula Divine Mermaid got to know the fauna. Sister Bea Wilder Mermaid walked the land. Every day she walked in a different direction, away from the Old Mermaid Sanctuary that the Old Mermaids were creating. She couldn't seem to stop walking. The other Old Mermaids admired her; she had gotten her land legs much faster than the others.

Yet at night, she still felt restless, and Sister DeeDee Lightful Mermaid—whom Sister Bea Wilder Mermaid loved best of all—and the other Old Mermaids couldn't seem to help her become restful. She walked and walked, day after day, until she came to the home of the Woman Who Loves Birds. Sister Bea

Wilder Mermaid had heard stories of the Woman Who Loves Birds, but she had never seen her before.

"Are you another lost explorer?" the Woman Who Loves Birds asked Sister Bea Wilder Mermaid when they first glimpsed each other as Sister Bea Wilder Mermaid came up over the rise.

"Just trying to figure out how this world works," Sister Bea Wilder Mermaid said.

"Ahhh, searching for the truth, then. Aren't you a little wet behind the ears for that?"

Sister Bea Wilder laughed. This woman was not going to talk about the weather.

"I heard you Old Mermaids had drifted this way," the Woman Who Loves Birds said. "Come on up and join me. Hot enough for you?"

The Woman Who Loves Birds told Sister Bea Wilder Mermaid to call her Annie as she brought her up to her house. Every step they took went past a bird house—all different shapes and sizes. Annie told Sister Bea Wilder Mermaid she found bits and pieces of the desert and brought them back here for the birds. "If it's got a hole and looks like it's a nice place to rest, I bring it back. Oh, look at that spider right there. See it? Hidden so nicely in this cactus."

Sister Bea Wilder Mermaid came and stood close to Annie and saw a web between two prickly pear pads. When she squinted, she could see the spider.

"How'd you know she was there?" Sister Bea Wilder Mermaid asked.

"I heard her spinning," Annie said. "Yep. I bet that's not

                    The First Book of

something you could hear in the Old Sea."

She started walking again. Then she stopped and sniffed the air. "You smell that?" she asked. "Ahhh, that's nectar to bats. They'll be feasting tonight." She pointed to a flowering agave.

"Smells like something rotten," Sister Bea Wilder Mermaid said.

"Perfume to the bats," Annie said. "I'll show you how to make something with a little kick to it from that one day. It'll have you howling at the moon."

"I do that already," Sister Bea Wilder Mermaid said.

"My kind of gal," Annie said.

It took them a long while to go down the path to Annie's house. Annie saw and heard and smelled so many things on the way there, and she pointed them all out to Sister Bea Wilder Mermaid. At first this stop-and-go pace was annoying to Sister Bea Wilder Mermaid. She was used to walking. She wanted to go, go, go. She was looking for something—she didn't know what—but it had to be up over that rise or around that corner or in the next moment, so she had to keep going. But now she walked slowly next to this Woman Who Loves Birds. It took them hours, days, weeks, to finally sit beneath a tall palo verde tree near her house.

The Woman Who Loves Birds gave Sister Bea Wilder Mermaid warm tea. They sipped the liquid together while they sat in the shade. The stillness throbbed around them. Sister Bea Wilder Mermaid listened to the bees in the palo verde. A rock squirrel came near her feet, picked up some bean pods, then wandered away. After a while, Sister Bea Wilder Mermaid began to feel the ground beneath her feet—truly feel it. It was different from the Old Sea, but it was there, touching her soles: solid, deep, stable. And the sky above her was different from the sky above the Old Sea, but it was the same sky. She breathed deeply.

After a while she began to notice the birds. First she heard the quail running beneath the shrubs and trees, cooing and clucking. Then she saw them. She chuckled. She wasn't sure why. The pear-shaped birds were just amusing to her. Then she saw a cactus wren. A raven. A mockingbird. A bright red cardinal. And hummingbirds. The hummingbirds were everywhere! It was said later—although we can't be sure this is true—that thousands of birds came to see this Old Mermaid who was sitting and drinking tea with the Woman Who Loves Birds. Sister Bea Wilder Mermaid squinted, or sighed, or something, and the birds either went about their business or were never there in that number to begin with. The hummingbirds lingered after the others had left, hovering in the air near Annie and Sister Bea Wilder Mermaid.

When the Woman Who Loves Birds and Sister Bea Wilder Mermaid had been sitting in silence and stillness for many moments or many moons, the Woman Who Loves Birds finally said, "Hummmm." And she sounded just like the hummingbirds. "Hummingbirds use spider webbing to hold their nests together, did you know that? Sometimes they use hair, too. I've seen them pull strands out from my brush. Their heart beats 500 times a minute, and that's when they're resting. I've counted. At night, they fluff their feathers and let all the heat out. Then they turn themselves off. It's like they're dead. In the morning, they come alive again."

"That must be something to see," Sister Bea Wilder Mermaid said.

"Yes, but then, isn't it all something to be?"

"Why do they call you the Woman Who Loves Birds?"

Annie shrugged. "They used to call me the Woman Who Loves Giants."

"Why?"

"Because I loved giants," she said. "Aren't you paying attention? Giants used to roam this place. Though, I guess you wouldn't say them roamed. Giants don't actually roam much. They trample. But they lived here and here abouts. Maybe thereabouts. The ones who lived here, those are the ones I loved. One in particular actually." She was quiet. "But that's another story."

"You had a falling out with the giants?"

"What do you mean?"

"Well, you aren't the Woman Who Loves Giants any more."

"Do you see any giants?" she asked.

Sister Bea Wilder Mermaid looked around. "No."

"They're here," she said. "They've just changed. Somehow. Some day. Some place. Maybe they got tired of being so earth bound. Maybe like you Old Mermaids got tired of the Old Sea."

"Well, that's not really what happened—"

"In any case." Annie motioned all around her, reminding Sister Bea Wilder Mermaid of the Old Woman and Old Man of the Mountains. "Now the giants are creatures of the air. I will say it is much easier to be a good host now that they're birds. They don't eat nearly as much as they did when they were giants."

Sister Bea Wilder Mermaid smiled. Then they sat in silence again for another week or more.

Sister Bea Wilder Mermaid and Annie became good friends. They often sat together, telling stories and sipping tea. More often they sat together and said nothing or sauntered the desert together. Annie seemed to know everything about everything, so Sister Bea Wilder Mermaid nicknamed her the Woman Who Knew Everything. Annie called her Sister Wild. Sometimes the other Old Mermaids came and visited with Annie, too.

After a time, Annie couldn't walk in the desert as much, so she and Sister Bea Wilder Mermaid sat together under the palo verde. Sister Bea Wilder Mermaid brought her pieces of wood and Annie carved little creatures out of them—mostly birds. Sometimes the piece of desert Sister Bea Wilder Mermaid brought her was so beautiful, she said it was already what it was intended to be, and she wasn't going to change that.

After she finished carving, she would place the finished bird on the small table next to her chair. The next day, the bird was always gone. One morning, Sister Bea Wilder Mermaid could have sworn she saw one of the carved birds shake itself and fly away, just like the hummingbirds coming alive again in the morning. Annie laughed when Sister Bea Wilder Mermaid told her what she had seen.

"You're getting desert eyes, Sister Wild," she said. "It's about time."

One day when Annie was not feeling well, Sister Bea

                                      The First Book of

Wilder Mermaid sat with her trying to coax her to eat some soup Sister Ruby Rosarita Mermaid had fixed her. Instead, Annie began to talk about her life.

"I miss the giants sometimes," Annie said. "I will admit that. I love the birds. I do. But sometimes I long to feel the Earth move like it did when the giants were tramping to and fro. And Mark, my giant, he was the biggest and the noisiest. And clumsy. I can't tell you how many trees he took down in his day." She shook her head. "He was something to see."

"Did he love you too?"

Annie smiled. "That sounds like something Sissy Maggie would ask. Of course he was very fond of me and I was very fond of him. But, it was not to be. It wouldn't have worked out."

"Sissy Maggie fell in love with the moon once," Sister Bea Wilder Mermaid said.

"And how did that work out?"

"Didn't," she said. "What happened to Mark?"

Annie shrugged. "He went wherever giants go when they die. Sometimes I imagine he's come back. I can feel the earth tremble and I see the trees sway and I know he's coming home. I even dreamed about it last night. He came and carried me off. It was great fun. I laughed the entire time." She smiled to herself. Then she looked at Sister Bea Wilder Mermaid and said, "Now, you know what to do when I'm gone?"

"No, what do you mean?"

"I've taught you everything I know," she said. "You know this desert now the way I know the desert, so you need to pass that knowledge on."

Sister Bea Wilder Mermaid shook her head. "I still can't hear a spider spinning. And I don't believe in giants."

"Hah! You do, too. You know, some people don't believe in Old Mermaids."

"Yeah, well, that's their loss," Sister Bea Wilder Mermaid said.

The Old Mermaid and the Woman Who Loved Giants sat together until the sun went down.

One night, Sister Bea Wilder Mermaid awakened because the earth was shaking. Or the house was shuddering. All the Old Mermaids got up and ran outside.

"This is what an earthquake feels like here," Sister Sophia Mermaid said.

The Old Mermaids agreed that must be what happened. But Sister Bea Wilder Mermaid wasn't so sure. As soon as the sun began to rise, she went over to Annie's house. The palo verde was missing a branch, and Annie's chair was on its side. Inside the house, Annie had taken her last breath.

Sister Bea Wilder Mermaid sat on her bed and cried for a long while. It was the Old Mermaid way of letting feelings flow. Later when she stepped outside and looked toward the mountains, it appeared that a path had been made between here and there. When she looked again, the path was gone. She righted the chair. A single tiny carved bird stood on the tiny table. Sister Bea Wilder Mermaid picked up the bird and put it gently in her pocket.

Later, the Old Mermaids scattered Annie's ashes in the desert. The wind blew the ashes this way and that. The birds watched, from everywhere. Sister Bea Wilder Mermaid knew

Annie would be pleased that she was now part of the earth.

Sister Bea Wilder Mermaid put the carved bird next to her bed and watched it for days, waiting for it to take flight. It never did. Sister Bea Wilder Mermaid kept it with her for almost always. It finally got lost in the wash somehow, sometime— which is how Myla ended up with it at the Church of the Old Mermaids—but Sister Bea Wilder Mermaid didn't need it any longer. She remembered her friend with every step she took, and she remembered her every time she sat still and listened. Sometimes she heard the birds. Sometimes she heard her heart-beat. Once she thought she heard a giant. Some say she even heard a spider spinning her web one afternoon. Some say she is still listening.

Tea Shell Offerings

Coyote Whispers Tea with Loco Honey

Mermaid Queens Bean Soup

Mountain Cinnamon Love BonBons

Nourishment

All the wisdom of the ages can be distilled
into one suggestion: Be.
>—*Mother Star Stupendous Mermaid*

Myla woke just after dawn. She got up and walked the wash alone. It was a damp and chilly morning. Dark clouds floated above the Rincons. A coyote walked across the wash. She stopped and looked at Myla. They stared at one another. Then the coyote continued on her way. Myla went back to the house and started breakfast. She sautéed onions and shitake mushrooms in olive oil.

As they sizzled she put on oatmeal. She sprinkled in a bit of cinnamon. Ernesto loved her oatmeal. She could not imagine why—probably had something to do with the almonds, cashews, bananas, and maple syrup he poured on it.

She cracked egg after egg into a bowl. Two eggs for each of them. She broke the yokes with a fork and whisked them.

The metal tines hit the inside of the bowl as she stirred them faster and faster, turning gold into more gold. As she poured the eggs into the pan with the mushrooms and onions, she thought, "This is the last breakfast I'll be making for the refugees at the Old Mermaids Sanctuary." She liked to think that the migrants came to the sanctuary as refugees but left as pilgrims. It was such a difficult decision to leave one's family and country—a desperate decision. How terrible then to be left in the desert to wander or die alone—or together with others as lost as you are.

Myla stared at the scrambled eggs as they began to set. She was glad she had dreamed of the Old Mermaids. It didn't really matter if she had originally dreamed of the Old Mermaids because of the mermaid tile or because she had seen David painting the mermaid. It didn't really matter if the Old Mermaids had been the voice of the Universe speaking to her. What mattered was that she had gone into the desert and helped people who needed it. In turn, they let her be a part of their families—their lives—for a time.

How could she ever have doubted the importance of that?

—from Church of the Old Mermaids

Sister Faye Mermaid and the Sleeping Beauties

ONE NIGHT AFTER the Old Mermaids washed ashore in the New Desert, Sister Faye Mermaid could not sleep. She wandered the half-finished house, gliding from room to room, like a ghost, a gentle breeze, or an Old Mermaid swimming in the Old Sea: She was quieter than a cactus mouse. Certainly quieter than the javelinas she smelled and heard snuffling around outside the house. Quieter than the coyotes yipping in the near distance. Maybe not as quiet as the jackrabbit she had seen under the saguaro up the ridge near the Hunter's place earlier in the day. Although maybe he wasn't so much quiet as absolutely still. Sister Faye Mermaid was not still. She was quiet. She did not wish to disturb any of the sleeping Old Mermaids.

After a time, Sister Faye Mermaid lay on the bench that curved out from the half-finished wall. She gazed up at the sky. *Stars, stars, everywhere; all without a care.* She shrugged. It wasn't much of a chant, certainly not a song. She sighed. She would miss being able to look up at the stars like this once the house was finished. Maybe she would talk to the others about putting in star windows. Sky windows. She liked that idea.

She watched the twinkling lights and listened to the sounds of the night desert. The house and the Old Mermaids breathed all around her, along with the trees, cacti, javelinas, coyotes, owls, and stars. She listened for an indication that the Invisibles were near. She watched the stars for some sign. Any kind of sign. She waited for a touch that would tell her the Invisibles were listening, that the Old Mermaids were not alone.

Sister Faye Mermaid got up again and stared into the milky darkness. She knew she and the Old Mermaids were not alone. My word! They were surrounded by the most interesting varieties of life—different from what they had known in the Old Sea, of course. But here Sister Faye Mermaid could not find any indication of Spirit, or the Invisibles, the Faeries. Perhaps she didn't know their language here—or the songs, the ceremonies. She did not know what she didn't know, but it was something. It was something that she had always known at any other place.

In the Old Sea, Sister Faye Mermaid had understood that the sigh of the East Wind meant cold and sometimes enlightenment was on the way. The West Wind most often brought storms and sometimes a sense of calamity. Or an upset stomach. She knew if an eel in the south canyon was wiggling out of its hole happily that either something good to eat was swimming by or it was time to celebrate. If she couldn't see even the tinniest glimmer of an eel's eye because it was so far back into its hole, she knew hard times were coming. (She hadn't seen an eel in an eon before the Old Sea dried up.) She knew by the way the sea fronds brushed up against her if the tide was coming in or out, and she understood all the implications of both. And always, always, she knew the great Old Sea listened to her chants and understood her questions.

Here. Here she didn't know which or what Invisibles she was talking to. If any. Maybe she was talking to Air. Which wasn't bad. Air gave her life. Gave them all life. Yet her conversations felt one-side. What songs did the New Desert Air want to hear? What did this place want from them?

Sister Faye Mermaid felt closed up and closed off and generally useless here. All the Old Mermaids had a purpose, they all had concrete skills—except her. Sister Ruby Rosarita was the best cook of them all. Sissy Maggie Mermaid made friends and made art. Sister Sheila Na Giggles could build or fix just about anything, all while she told a joke or a story. Sister Ursula Divine Mermaid understood the fauna; Sister Bea Wilder Mermaid understand the land. Sister Laughs A Lot and Sister Bridget Mermaid knew all the plants. Sister Sophia Mermaid had the wisdom of the ages in her brain and all through her body. They all had something. And before Sister Faye Mermaid had always been able to synthesize their collective wisdom and act as a kind of negotiator and go-between for the Old Mermaids and the geni loci of a place.

A while back, Sister Faye Mermaid had decided she needed to do something physical to get herself back into the shape she had been before. She went up to Annie's house and asked to take a bath in her big old tub. She figured once her body was immersed in water, she'd fill up with herself again and all would be well. She wouldn't let Annie heat up the water—she thought that was just strange—so it came as a shock to her that the water was a shock to her. She ended up sitting in the tub shivering. When she finally got out of the tub, she looked down at her body and was startled to see herself—truly—for the first time since she had left the Old Sea.

She said, "I ain't what I used to be."

Maybe that meant she couldn't do what she had been able to do before. She felt anchored. Trapped. She remembered feeling adrift. Ahhhh. Freedom.

Sister Faye Mermaid had talked to the others about how she felt. Sister Sophia Mermaid said, "Many religious and spiritual traditions suggest a time of solitude or fasting might be in order. Or you might try a hallucinogenic. The desert is full of them."

Mother Star Stupendous Mermaid said, "Perhaps we were meant for the desert all along. Maybe the Old Sea was just a preparation for this."

"Who meant us for this then?" Sister Faye Mermaid asked.

"Maybe we did."

"We aren't who we were," Sister Faye Mermaid said.

"I know," Mother Star Stupendous Mermaid said. "Isn't that grand?"

Now Sister Faye Mermaid wandered into the front room. She gazed at the wall where Sissy Maggie Mermaid had painted a mountain scene. Even in the darkness, Sister Faye Mermaid could see and feel the presence of the mountain. It was as if she could walk right into it. On the opposite wall was a scene from the Old Sea. She didn't want to get too close to it right now. She was afraid she might hear the ocean, might walk into the painting and never come back.

She turned away from the mountain scene. The night was beginning to gray into dawn. She had spent another night sleepless. And she had learned nothing. No secrets. No geni loci had made themselves known to her. She began walking from room to room again. Grand Mother Yemaya Mermaid snored softly in her room. Next door Mother Star Stupendous lay on her side with her hands together under her face. She looked peaceful, beautiful.

In the next room, Sister DeeDee Lightful Mermaid and Sister Bea Wilder Mermaid curled up around one another. Nearby Sissy Maggie Mermaid and Sister Laughs A Lot Mermaid had fallen asleep next to one another. Earlier the four of them had been planning Sissy Maggie Mermaid's next art project. Sissy Maggie Mermaid had snuggled up to Sister Laughs A Lot Mermaid, just like they used to when they were young, sunning themselves with a group of walruses near the shore. A lock of Sister Laughs A Lot Mermaid's hair had fallen down near her eyes, in a curl that looked like a seahorse's tail. Something about that made Sister Faye Mermaid's breath catch in her throat. Her chest ached. She smiled and kept herself from brushing the hair off of Sister Laughs A Lot Mermaid's face. She suddenly felt adrift. Ahhhh.

It had been a long while since she had realized how beautiful they all were—even though they weren't what they used to be. It had been a long time since she acknowledged how glad she was that she had washed up onto this desert with these Old Mermaids.

Just then Sister Laughs A Lot Mermaid opened her eyes sleepily. "Oh, it's you. I thought I heard you singing."

"I wasn't singing, sweetheart," Sister Faye Mermaid whispered. "I was just breathing."

"Same thing." Sister Laughs A Lot Mermaid closed her eyes and was asleep again.

Sister Faye Mermaid turned and stepped over the wall and walked into the morning desert. A beam of sunlight illuminated a spot under the palo verde tree near the house. Sister Faye Mermaid stared at it. The spot was gold and green and comforting and wild, and she kept still, so still, so she could breathe in the mystery of it all. The desert breathed with her. The spot breathed with her. Then the spot turned its head. Sister Faye Mermaid was looking directly into two eyes filled with sunlight.

She blinked, not understanding what she was seeing. Two tufted ears. This was how the desert faeries looked, according to Annie, The Woman Who Loves Birds. Sister Faye Mermaid heard herself singing. Had she been singing all along? The spot got up and moved out of the light. Something or someone shifted. The desert faery was really a bobcat—or the other way around—and it was looking directly at her as if to say, "You called me. Now what?" The bobcat slowly walked away. It stopped and looked back at Sister Faye Mermaid. She grinned. She couldn't wait to tell the others. *Later*. She'd let sleeping beauties sleep for now. The bobcat desert faery disappeared; Sister Faye Mermaid followed.

The Thirteen Suggestions

Get the starfish outta your eyes, sister.
Sister Sheila Na Giggles Mermaid

Step lightly. Dance hard. Eat your vegetables.
Sister DeeDee Lightful Mermaid

Things change. Get over it.
Sister Bea Wilder Mermaid

Fear has no sisters, but I have many.
Sister Lyra Musica Mermaid

She who laughs a lot laughs a lot.
Sister Laughs A Lot Mermaid

I am most at home where the wild things are.
Sister Ursula Divine Mermaid

Sing, dance, create. If you have to choose one, do all three at once.
Sister Bridget Mermaid

A good bean is hard to find. Everything else is easy.
Sister Ruby Rosarita Mermaid

Go with the flow—and watch out for waterfalls.
Sister Sophia Mermaid

You ask me to tell you about love? Showing is so much better.
Sister Magdelene Mermaid

Laugh or weep. We swim in your tears.
Grand Mother Yemaya Mermaid

All the wisdom of the ages can be distilled into one suggestion: Be.
Mother Star Stupendous Mermaid

The rest is . . . mystery.
Sister Faye Mermaid

KIM ANTIEAU IS the author of *The Fish Wife, Church of the Old Mermaids, The Blue Tail, Coyote Cowgirl, The Jigsaw Woman, The Salmon Mysteries,* and many other novels, stories, poems, and essays. She lives in the Pacific Northwest and the desert Southwest. Learn more about Kim and her work at www.kimantieau.com.